HIS GAME

BY

ANGEL RAYNE

His Game
Copyright © Angel Rayne 2022
All Rights Reserved

Published by Everblood Publishing, LLC
https://everbloodpublishing.com

ISBN-13: 9781945499586

Cover Design by Coffee and Characters

Copy Editor: Jinxie Gervasio @ jinxiesworld.com

Proofreader: Mackenzie @ NiceGirlNaughtyEdits.com

ALSO BY ANGEL RAYNE

Mafia Romance Reading Order

Luca and Veda

His Game

His Stakes

His Win

SYNOPSIS

She tries to escape.
She tries to reason with me.
And then she tries to change the rules.
But this is *my* game, and I won't be played. I own
her now...

Three years ago, I let down my guard, and I paid the
ultimate price when the woman I loved was murdered
right in front of my eyes.

I have a chance to make it right. To earn back the respect
of my father and my place in the family as the underboss.
A way to finally take my revenge on the bastard who took
her away...

By stealing his fiancée.

Veda is a means to an end, a weakness I can't afford to
have, and I'm *obsessed* with having her.

If I was a decent man, I would let her go.
But I am not that kind of man.

My heart stopped, my soul lifting from my body, and I didn't give two fucks if I died right here on this ripped up, old couch as my orgasm slid down my spine, tightening my balls before rushing through my cock. My back arched and my sex pulsed with every ejaculation, my hoarse cry echoing off the barren walls of what used to be a break room.

The woman astride me threw back her head with abandon. "Luca!"

The ends of her long, black hair brushed my thighs as she rode my sex with desperate undulations of her hips, milking every last drop out of me. I palmed her large breasts, greedily soaking in the sight of the ample flesh spilling out of my hands, the dark nipples straining against my palms. But much as I'd love to stay here with her for another round or two, we needed to wrap things up and get back out to the warehouse to oversee the narcotics exchange between her people and mine.

The mafia and the cartel had never gotten along so well.

When I had nothing left to give her, neither a shred of my heart nor a drop of my cum, she lifted her head and looked down at me with a lazy smile, her dark eyes dancing with the joy of being alive. Something icy and hard cracked within my chest, and I felt the corners of my mouth lift in response to her awestruck gaze. My Maria...so fucking beautiful...I was going to fucking marry her. My father might not approve. But as the boss, he would have to see it would be a good alliance.

Pop!

Blood splattered across my face, neck, and chest, getting in my mouth and eyes. Blinking hard, I stared up at her smiling face as the sparkle faded from her brown eyes and her life trickled from the single hole in the center of her forehead. And even though I watched it happen, even though she was right there in front of my fucking eyes, it took me a full three seconds to comprehend what I had just witnessed.

"Maria!" The salty copper taste of her blood coated my tongue, a horrifying contradiction to the sweet taste of her pussy. "Fuck. Fuck...MARIA!" I roared out her name.

Pop! Pop! Pop!

Slugs hit the couch around me with a dull thud, each one pushing me to snap out of it. To fucking move. Acting on pure instinct, I slid off the couch to the floor, keeping her lifeless body between my most vital organs and the shooter who stood at the end of the couch, slightly to the left. I felt her body jerk as a bullet went through her shoulder and into the floor beside my head, grazing my ear.

Reaching for my pants, I tried to pull them toward me while keeping myself as close to the couch as I could. It wasn't much of a shield, but it was something. My holster and gun were lying on top of my clothes, if I could just reach them. Keeping my eyes right where someone would appear at the end of the couch and my ears open for footsteps, I slammed a door down on my emotions, sliding easily back into the role of cold-blooded killer. Maybe too easily. The man I was before I'd met her. The man my father had forced me to become. Unfeeling. More dead than alive.

The monster I would unleash once again to avenge her death.

I could feel him clawing at my ribcage. Hear him roaring with rage in my head. My heart slowed to a steady rhythm. My focus became razor sharp. Later, I would mourn the woman I loved. Right now, I just had to keep myself alive.

My fingertips finally touched cold metal and I smiled. This motherfucker was a dead man. Gun in hand, I shoved Maria off of me and crab walked backward, my bare feet sliding on the blood that had dripped to the concrete floor, squeezing myself between the wall and the other end of the couch. Squatting on the balls of my feet, I leaned out and took a quick look toward the doorway, aiming right where the fucker's head would be.

No one was there.

Uncaring of the fact that I was as naked as the day I was born, I stood up and strode to the doorway, throwing my back against the wall. Again, I listened.

A whistle echoed down the hall.

"Gotta go! Gotta go!"

Footsteps ran down the hall, and from the sound of them, I could tell he or she was running away from this room. Away from me.

I stuck my head out of the doorway, pulling it back just in time to avoid being shot in the face as the shooter tried to keep me where I was so he could make his getaway.

But that was okay. I'd seen what I'd needed to see. Even if I didn't believe it.

Shutting down the rage and confusion that tightened my chest, I gave my head a fierce shake and got myself back in the game. I needed to stay alive now more than ever. I had to warn the family.

Quickly and silently, I returned to where Maria lay sprawled across the floor, her limbs bent at unnatural angles in my haste to get out from underneath her. I picked up her body and laid her on the couch, carefully this time, keeping one eye on the door in case anyone was stupid enough to come back as I dragged on only my pants, not bothering with my shirt or suit jacket, which I laid over her to preserve her modesty. "I'll be back to get you, *amore*," I told her, then kissed her on the cheek. My lips left a bloody print on her flawless brown skin, and I ran my thumb through it, smearing it toward her ear.

Barefoot, I crept silently down the hall to the main part of the warehouse. Low voices murmured something I couldn't make out. Then I heard movement. Lots of movement. But I wasn't so stupid as to make my presence known before I knew what I was dealing with.

Slowly, I slid my shoulder down the wall until I sat on my heels where no one would expect to see me, then quickly looked out around the corner, gun pointed low. The feds swarmed the place like locusts, busting open crates and sweeping the place with drug dogs. My soldiers and Maria's men were rounded up and cuffed near the loading dock. And the prick who shot my Maria was talking to one of the agents. I didn't fucking miss the fact he wasn't handcuffed. As I watched, he glanced back over his shoulder toward the hallway where I was, as though he felt me watching him.

Motherfucker.

Rising to my full height, I jogged back down the hall to the break room, my bare feet silent on the hard floors.

A man was standing over Maria's body. He held my shirt up away from her body, and he was staring at her tits. Without thinking, I lifted my gun, aiming where his face will be in about two seconds. "You're a sick fuck. You know that?"

His head shot up, and I noticed his eyes were such a light blue they appeared almost white, right before I stuck a bullet between them. It was almost comical, the way his head flew back on his neck but his body remained as it was for a few seconds before it finally caught up with the program and he collapsed to the floor.

Gun still in my palm, I pressed my hands to the top of my head and paced. "Think," I told myself out loud. "Think, you fucker."

But there was nothing I could fucking do to save the deal. At least not at this moment. I'd been stupid. Too worried about getting my dick wet to see the signs. So fucking certain I had everything under control.

Grabbing my cell off the table, I picked up my shoes and prepared for the phone call I would have to make to my father to tell him what had happened. He wasn't going to be happy with me.

But first I had to get the hell out of here. Preferably without the escort that was going to start looking for me any fucking moment. I knew before I shot their comrade they would hear the shot, but he was fucking disrespecting the woman I loved. And I couldn't allow him to get away with that shit.

Closing the door, I locked it and shoved my gun into the back of my pants, then pushed a metal file cabinet in front of it. It wouldn't hold them off for long, but hopefully it would be enough time that I could get the hell out of here. Eyeing the opposite wall, I rushed to the other side of the room, busted the glass out of the old window that had been painted shut, then slammed my palms down on the jagged edges. Sticking my arms out the window, I shook them outside, leaving just enough blood laying around to throw them off.

With a whispered, "Forgive me, *amore*," I took my shirt from Maria's body, ripped it in half, and wrapped it around my bleeding hands. Then I squeezed into the corner between another, taller, file cabinet and the wall just as there was a horrible screeching noise and the door burst open.

I watched two agents run into the room. One of them ran straight for the busted window while the other scanned the room, weapon drawn, before checking the bodies and then holstering his weapon and joining his friend at the window. He called it in on his radio as they hustled out of the room.

Once they were gone, I went to the door, checking that no one else was coming before I snuck out and jogged down the hall in the opposite direction. There was another room down here with a back door. If I could make it without being seen, I could hide along the road until Enzo came and got me. He always stayed close by during these deals, for this exact reason.

Pulling out my cell phone, I texted him, then pushed open the door and ran out into the night.

I was banned from attending Maria's funeral in Mexico, and as such, the surprise on her brother's face was expected when I walked up to stand beside him in the living room where his sister's body was laid out. The house was crowded with family and friends, talking and laughing and praying, and the smell of tamales permeated the room, making my stomach growl. But I couldn't bring myself to eat. "I'm so sorry," I told him. "This never should have happened, Rene."

"No, *estúpido*. It shouldn't have," he responded in his heavy accent. Hands clasped in front of him, he watched his mother as she leaned over the casket, speaking rapid Spanish to her oldest daughter, now deceased because of me.

Something strange and foreign clenched in my chest, and I had to clear my throat before I could speak. "I donated fifty thousand dollars to your family's church," I told him. "I know it won't bring her back, but I wanted to do something."

"My mother will appreciate the sentiment."

"But not you?"

"I haven't been to church in years, my friend. If I tried to go now, I'm afraid I might burst into flame the moment I walk through the doors." He tossed me a grin, strained with grief.

I stared straight ahead in the direction of the coffin, not really seeing it, though. "If you want to shoot me, I'll understand. And no one will stop you. Or blame you. I came here alone."

I felt his eyes on me. "You've got some balls, *puto*, that's for sure," he said. Then he sighed. "The thought has crossed my mind. More than once. But then I thought to myself, 'Luca loved my sister. Truly loved her. He would never have let this happen if he could've stopped it.' And I put my gun away."

His mother moved away from the coffin, and my love's perfect face came into view, her dark hair neatly combed until it lay silky and straight on the white silk pillow, unlike how I was used to seeing it, in wild disarray. A wave of something dark and desperate erupted inside of me, and I swayed on my feet. "I do love her," I told him, my voice thick with tears I couldn't shed. "I wanted to marry her, Rene."

"She would've been so happy," he said after a moment.

I took some time to get myself under control before I could get the rest of this out. "This...this was my fault."

"No, Luca. You couldn't have known this would happen."

Despite his words, I kept going, knowing if I stopped, I'd never be able to get it all out. "I was distracted, Rene. I let down my guard." I didn't tell him that I had lost focus because I was too eager to see her. Or what we were doing when it happened. Although he could probably guess if he knew she was found naked in the back room. "This was my fault," I repeated. "But I will make it right."

Rene stood stiffly beside me, and I thought for a moment he was going to take me up on my offer and pull out his gun after all. And if that's what he felt needed to be done,

I would respect his decision. I wouldn't run. Or defend myself. It was his right as her brother.

Finally, he said quietly, "You find the *pendejo* that killed my little sister, and you make him suffer as you have suffered, Luca. As I have suffered. You take away the thing he loves most in the world. And then I will forgive you."

There was only one problem with this demand. Up until a week ago, I thought *I* was the thing her murderer loved the most.

Yet, I gave him a nod, walked up to the casket, and kissed my Maria one last time. Her lips were cold and hard. The passion that had burned within her and set fire to everyone lucky enough to be in the vicinity extinguished forever. "I will see you again, *amore*," I whispered in her ear, and then I turned and walked out of the house.

*T*HREE *Y*EARS *Later*

"LUCA. TURN ON THE TV."

I glanced up from my book to see Enzo, my best friend since grade school—now my right-hand man—entering my study. He hadn't even taken his coat off yet. "You're dripping all over my floor."

Removing his ever-present sunglasses, even with the storm raging outside, his mouth twisted with impatience.

He found the remote near the television and turned it on, flipping through channels until he found a blonde woman in a revealing blue dress being interviewed by a daytime talk show host. She had a pretty, slightly heart-shaped face with wide-set blue eyes, a straight nose, and lips like Scarlett Johansson.

"Who is this?" I asked. "And why do I care?"

"Shhh. Listen." He turned up the volume.

"So," the interviewer said. "I heard from a little bird that you recently got engaged."

The blonde smiled, tilting her face away with a fake show of shyness that anyone with half a brain would see right through. "I did," she whispered in a conspiring tone as the camera zoomed in on her. I noticed her pupils were enlarged. From too many prescription drugs, would be my guess.

"Can we get a name for this mystery man?" The interviewer leaned in closer, like they were a couple of best girlfriends telling each other secrets.

"Well, I'm not supposed to say. But I'm just so excited!"

"I promise I won't tell anyone," the interviewer told her, her eyes bright with curiosity.

The blonde gave her a coy look. Her name flashed across the bottom of the screen—Nicole Calbert, actress. I'd never seen her in any films, but that didn't mean anything. Perhaps she was in television or on the stage. I didn't watch much television or frequent the theaters. "His name is Mario. Mario Morel—"

The screen went black for a few seconds. And when the show came back on, Nicole was gone from the chair and the interviewer was apologizing for the disruption, her eyes wide and her shoulders tense, claiming her guest had suffered from a sudden illness. The show cut off, and a news anchor recapped the clip we'd just watched, ending with the question, "Was it really a nauseous stomach? Or a case of diarrhea of the mouth that ended this interview so quickly?"

My man Enzo turned off the television.

I steepled my fingers, my mind racing as fast as my heart. "So, where has my brother been all of this time?"

"Witness protection," Enzo said.

It was what we had assumed after what had gone down at the warehouse when Maria was killed. What I'd seen with my own two eyes. But I didn't understand. "Why is he back? He has to know I've been looking for him. The entire family has. He has a target on his back a mile wide."

He just shrugged. "We don't know."

My brother was a rat. I had no idea why he was risking his life by coming back here, and I decided I didn't really give a fuck. The fact was he was here, and I needed to get to him before anyone else did. This was *my* game. "Find that woman," I told him, a plan already forming. "Now."

"Tristan is already on it. Mark's wife saw the interview happen in real time and told him about it as soon as she realized what that actress had been about to say. He told Tristan and Tristan told me."

And this was why they were my guys.

Three days later, my car was parked in a lot across the street from a brand new, seventeen-story building in the Market District of downtown Austin. The condos here were said to run upward of five thousand a month for a studio. An amount I—or a successful actress—wouldn't blink at, but something told me she hadn't chosen this location as much as been placed in it. Mario and his men frequented this area of the city. Or, at least, he had before he went into witness protection. And before I began to hunt him like the fucking traitor he was.

"Are you sure this is the correct location?" I asked from the backseat of the SUV. This whole thing made me nervous. Mario had been gone for years. Why the hell would he come back here? And why now? He had to know that I would find out the moment he stepped foot in my city again.

"This is the last known address of Nicole Calbert. Her rent was paid in full for an entire year just last month," Tristan said.

"It looks like the kind of place Mario would set up one of his women," Enzo commented.

"But you haven't actually seen her yet?"

"No," he told me. "Tris and I have been camped out here for the last two days while you've been dealing with that delivery issue, and nothing yet."

I took a sip of my coffee, my eyes on the door of the building.

We'd been here for an hour, and I was just about to tell Tristan to forget about it and take me home when a woman approached from the east on the opposite side of the street. Her hair wasn't as bleached, and she was dressed rather casually in a pair of black shorts, a pink tank top with some kind of colored pattern on the front, and flip-flops, but there was no mistaking that pretty face.

Tristan saw her at the same time as I did and held up his phone, zooming in to take some photos.

"Is that her?" Enzo asked.

"It sure as hell looks like her," he said. "The hair is different."

"That doesn't mean anything," Enzo told him. "Women are like chameleons these days. A different color for every day of the week."

I opened the car door and got out.

"Whoa. Whoa. Wait. Luca! Where the fuck are you going?" Enzo jumped out of the car and jogged around the front, one hand slipping inside of his jacket to rest on the handle of his gun as he quickly cased the area. "What are you doing?" he asked when he came to stand beside me. I ignored his questions as I buttoned my suit jacket. It was already hot, waves of heat coming up from the pavement. My shirt would be stuck to my back by the time I made it across the street, but I couldn't very well walk around with my gun in plain sight without drawing attention.

"It's all right," I told him. "Get back in the car."

"Luca, no. It's too dangerous. This wasn't part of the plan."

He was right. But I needed to see for myself. "I just want to make sure it's her. I'll be right back." Checking for cars, I jogged across the street and got into position to intercept her, blending in with a group of office workers heading to the nearest coffee shop or whatever they did on their breaks these days.

As I got closer, I saw she was wearing earbuds and my eyes narrowed. The easiest way to get assaulted was to not be aware of your surroundings. Dragging my attention from her flawless face, prettier than I remembered, I saw her tank top had a multi-colored peace sign on the front, and the hem of her shorts was frayed in places. A fashion choice? Or was she a woman who didn't feel the need to impress every time she was out in public. That wasn't the impression I'd gotten from her television appearance.

I sped up my steps so I would reach the door of the building at the same moment she did. She paid no attention to me as I suddenly broke off from the group, pretending to look down at my phone. I stepped into her path and reached for the door handle, acting surprised when she crashed into my right side.

"Oh! I'm so sorry!" Startled, she jumped back so fast she lost her footing.

Her soft voice rippled over my skin, touching me as intimately as a woman's fingers. I reached out and grabbed her around the waist with one arm as she flailed backwards, then helped her to right herself. Her skin was warmed from the sun beneath her shirt, and my grip on her tightened instinctively before I remembered myself and let her go.

She took a step back and lifted her hands to brush her hair out of her face. I inhaled, preparing to speak, and her scent drifted over me. I froze, my entire body from the top of my head to the soles of my feet suddenly tightened with need. I'd expected some type of cloying perfume or flowery lotion, but she only smelled clean and slightly like fresh oranges...and her own natural musk, sweeter than anything made in a lab.

She stared up at me with those wide eyes, and I saw they were gray, not as blue as they'd appeared on the television. "Thank you," she said a little too loudly. I tried to hear what she was listening to, but the constant traffic and construction drowned out everything else. "And again, I'm so sorry."

Unsettled by my reaction to her, I found it difficult to respond right away. Her pleasant expression faltered, and she looked away, shifting her weight from one foot to the other as she waited for me to get out of the way. "No," I finally said, giving myself an internal shake, "please accept my apologies. I wasn't watching where I was going."

The corners of her mouth turned up as she pulled an earbud out of her ear. "Sorry, but I didn't hear a word you just said." She had only the tiniest hint of a southern accent. Which told me she hadn't been born here, but had acquired it after living in Texas for many years.

That little tease of a smile was one of the sexiest things I'd ever seen. After a moment, I said, "I was apologizing. It was my fault we ran into each other. I had my eyes on my phone." I paused, then reached for the door handle and pulled it open for her. "Allow me."

"Thank you," she said simply, and stuck her earbud back in as she flounced past me and into the building, her sandals flapping loudly in the cavernous foyer.

I didn't follow her.

I would see her again soon enough.

CHAPTER 1

VEDA

"Nicole, get your scraggly ass out here right now! You bitch!"

I screamed the words into the empty foyer, listening for a response as they echoed through the sparsely furnished rooms of my twin sister's fancy new downtown condo, and not surprised when I didn't receive one. This was the third time I'd been here in the past week, and every time I had to come back, I only got more and more pissed off.

When there was still no answer, I shut the front door and laid my spare key on the overpriced marble table—I wouldn't be needing it anymore—and narrowed my eyes at the obnoxious vase of flowers she kept there just because she knew I was allergic to them.

Right on cue, I sneezed. With a snarl, I grabbed the vase, stalked as well as I could in my flip-flops across the main room to the patio doors that led out to the balcony, flung them open, and nearly chucked the entire thing over the railing. But the blast of Texas heat made me pause at the last minute and gave me time to rethink what I was about to do. Taking the flowers out of the vase, I threw them over, then dropped the vase on the patio, smiling as it smashed into tiny shards of glass. "Oops." After all, if I dropped a crystal vase fifteen floors down, I'd probably kill someone, and I really didn't want that on my conscience, even if I didn't get caught.

I went back into the air-conditioned condo and shut the doors again, muting the sounds of the city down below and the likely tirade that would be aimed at me when a cluster of daisies and carnations landed on someone's head.

Dusting the pollen off my hands, I felt a surge of satisfaction. I was done being my sister's errand runner, grocery shopper, and whatever the hell else Nicole deemed herself too rich and famous to do for herself. I'd been doing it since she got her first acting job two years ago, and as she got more and more offers for jobs, and more and more full of herself, I'd wanted to quit many times. But I didn't. Because she was my fucking sister.

But this last demand of hers...ha! This, I would not do.

Reaching into the front pocket of the artfully ripped jean shorts I'd scored at Goodwill, I pulled out the invitation I'd gotten in the mail earlier this week. It was covered in some kind of loopy calligraphy that I eventually interpreted to be Nicole's way of ordering me to be her maid of honor in her upcoming nuptials. Where she would marry someone I, her very own sister, had never met and that I'd known absolutely nothing about until I'd received the invitation. A wedding I probably wouldn't have even been invited to if it wasn't for the fact that I was her *only* sister, and that at least one of our parents would be pissed enough to cut her off from the family if she didn't offer me this exalted position.

Done. I am so fucking done.

"Nicole!" I yelled again, just in case she was ignoring me. Popping my head into her bedroom, I scanned the rumpled king-sized bed with the gaudy yellow comforter —I *hated* yellow—before walking over to the bathroom. My sister was nowhere to be found, so I wandered back out to the kitchen and grabbed a wineglass and a bottle of something that was on the very bottom rack of her wine fridge—which meant she was saving it for a special occasion. Pulling my cell out of my back pocket, I sat down and set my phone on the couch cushion beside me, poured myself a glass of wine, turned on the TV, and put my dusty flip-flops up on her spotless coffee table. And I intended to park my ass right there until the bitch came home.

Or until I ran out of wine and needed another bottle. Or a bathroom.

Images flashed across the television screen, but I had no idea what I was watching. All I kept thinking about was how heartbroken our father would be when he found out I'd disowned my sister, but I needed a change. I needed my own life.

My mother, however...well, she probably wouldn't even notice I wasn't coming around anymore. She'd always preferred my older sister over me. Nicole was the child she'd planned on having. I...was not.

I was the unexpected twin with the damaged heart that was never supposed to have happened. Because we were premature, I was born with a patent ductus arteriosus (or PDA). Luckily, the hole was small, and a simple surgery closed the opening between the two major blood vessels leading from my heart, leaving me with two very faint, very small scars under my left arm that were barely visible now. And other than periodic checkups with my cardiologist, I've lived a normal life. My mother, however, had wanted to adopt me out and only keep the healthy baby, but my father somehow managed to talk her out of it. One of the few times he'd been successful at that. How did I know this? Because my mother told me this right to my face when I was thirteen years old.

And honestly, after twenty-two years of feeling nothing from my mother but apathy, I wished he'd have let her do it. Because even though the doctors fixed my heart, I've never been good enough for my mother, no matter how hard I'd tried. My grades were never as good as Nicole's. I was never coordinated enough to be a cheerleader like Nicole. I didn't know how to act around our parent's high society friends, while Nicole could charm them with nothing but a smile and a flip of her bleached, white-blonde hair. Nicole's best friend was the daughter of a man who owned a multi-million-dollar company and invited the entire family out on his yacht. My best friend for the last fifteen years was Sammy, a black lesbian, which of course had to mean I was gay, too. I wasn't, but my mother refused to believe me. And to her, having a daughter who wasn't a "normal" woman was a personal affront to her family's good breeding. I'd spent my entire life feeling like I wasn't worthy. Like I wasn't "as good as."

Trying to get away from my dark thoughts, I took a large gulp of my sister's expensive wine, but I barely tasted the different notes of cherry and chocolate or how smooth it was on my tongue, because no matter how much I tried to run away from it, I was beginning to think my mother was right. I'd barely graduated high school. Never went to college—not because I couldn't afford it, which was true, but because I just didn't want to. I could get jobs, but had a hard time keeping them, either because I got bored or I got fired. And if Nicole hadn't hired me to be her lackey, I probably would've ended up out on the street by now.

However, that didn't mean I had to put up with my sister's abuse anymore. Every word she directed toward me, every little thing she conned me into doing for her, every time she looked down her nose at me...

No. I was fucking done. I might not be as charming as her, or as smart as her, or even as sexy as her—because I was a bit "thicker" as Mom loved to remind me, despite the fact we were identical twins—but I was worth something to somebody. Somewhere.

And maybe if I got the hell away from my sister, I'd start believing that.

I heard the click of the front door and swung my head in that direction, frowning as I waited for the room to right itself again. Maybe the wine hadn't been such a good idea. But then again, maybe it would give me the courage to say what I had to say without giving Nicole the opportunity to make me doubt my own words, as she tended to do.

Setting my wine glass next to the nearly empty bottle, I got to my feet and unconsciously pushed back my shoulders and raised my chin. Taking a deep breath, I turned to face my only sibling, my twin, who I both loved and hated in equal measure. Well, maybe like sixty/forty.

Seventy/thirty?

I waited to hear the heels she always wore clacking across the stained concrete floors as she waltzed into the room with her usual air of self-importance, arms full of shopping bags since it was Saturday and she always shopped on the weekends unless she was on set. When I didn't hear anything, I sidestepped my way out from between the couch and the coffee table and walked over to the center of the room so I could see the front door.

A tall, good-looking man with dark hair and a short beard stood just out of view of where I'd been sitting. He was wearing a tailored, nondescript suit that would easily blend in with all of the other businessmen working in the city. Behind him was another man dressed much the same, only his black hair stuck straight up on his head. Sunglasses hid his eyes and a five o'clock shadow covered his hard jaw. He was even taller than the other guy. Neither one looked surprised to see me.

Could one of these guys be the fiancé I'd yet to meet?

My normal cautious nature dulled by the wine, I threw my hands in the air as if to say, "Finally!", smiled, and walked toward them. When I got close enough to shake the hand of the first one, I opened my mouth to introduce myself to my new brother-in-law...

And had a piece of cloth stuffed into it. Before I could spit it out or get my limbs to coordinate with what my brain was trying to tell me to do, suit number two was behind me, tying a gag around my head. My fight-or-flight instinct didn't fully kick in until a black hood was pulled down over my face. When my arms were pulled behind my back, I threw my body weight into the guy behind me, throwing him off balance as I kicked out at the one in front of me. My flip-flop met nothing but empty air though, and I was caught before I could fall to the floor and get the hood off my head.

"I didn't want to do this," one of them muttered.

A hand came up under my hood and a cloth was pressed to my nose and mouth. It smelled sweet and slightly like chemicals, and I tried to breathe through my mouth, but the gag made it impossible. I moaned as my head began to swim.

And then I knew nothing else.

CHAPTER 2
LUCA

I turned from the wall of glass that made up the back of my home and watched as Enzo—one of the only two people I trusted most in the world—carried in Mario's new fiancée and laid her carefully on my black leather couch. Anyone who saw how gently he handled her would think he actually had a heart beating in that chest, but I knew better.

I finished the whiskey in my hand and set the glass down on the small coffee table in the center of the group of chairs that made up the sitting area, ignoring the twinge of disloyalty in my chest. "Did anyone see you?" I asked him.

Enzo took off his sunglasses—his way of showing respect —and shook his head. "Nah. We're good."

"Are you absolutely sure about that? Not even our own guards outside? Or Mario's? No one can know she's here just yet."

He gave me a sharp nod. "I made sure of it."

"And Tristan..."

"Took the car to get cleaned."

I grunted my approval. When Mario figured out she was gone, he would stop at nothing to find her. Not because he loved her, but because he hated having anything he considered his taken from him. We were much alike in that way. And I had no doubt he'd eventually figure out exactly where his precious bride-to-be had gone, but not until I wanted him to. Not until I was ready. Not until Nicole Calbert was loyal to me.

And only me.

I pulled my cell phone out of my inside jacket pocket and called my father, the only other person who knew about my plan, as we didn't want this to get out to the rest of the family just yet. He answered on the second ring. "I've got her," I told him before he could say anything.

"Any witnesses?"

"No."

"Good." He hung up.

I slid my phone back into my pocket and picked up my whiskey glass, raising it halfway to my lips before I remembered it was empty and set it back on the counter, the underlying tone in my father's voice ringing in my ears. Running my finger along the rim of my glass, I was careful not to show my emotions to Enzo, although he knew me well enough that hiding anything from him was near impossible.

My father expected me to fuck this up. And after what had happened the last time I'd dealt with Mario, I didn't blame him. But what he didn't know was that I'd been planning this revenge for years. Fucking *years*. Watching. Waiting. Biding my time and planning every single tiny detail. I'd just been waiting for her.

I would not fail my father again.

My jaw began to ache, and I rolled my head on my neck to ease the tension, then turned back to the woman on the couch. My eyes traveled down her body, exposed as it was by how little she was wearing, the jean shorts and grungy T-shirt looking like she'd pulled them out of a donation bin. She was just as I remembered from the last time I'd seen her, only five days before, small compared to myself and Enzo, tan, curvy...all legs, hips, and tits. A body that deserved to be wrapped in the finest silks and cashmere, not cheap, threadbare cotton.

Her hand twitched, and a muffled moan came from beneath the hood obscuring her face. Curious if she was really as stunning as the recollection of her that had haunted me this last week, I walked over and grabbed a handful of the material and yanked it from her head, thinking I had to be wrong. Women with bodies like that rarely had a face that matched.

Long hair the color of pale wheat tumbled about her face in static-y waves, sticking to her forehead and cheeks, and all I could really see were her pink stained lips stretched wide around the gag. Blood rushed to my groin as I imagined those lips wrapped around my cock. Reaching beneath my suit jacket, I pulled my favorite knife from its shoulder holster. But just as I got the tip near her face, her eyes fluttered open, shades of gray peeking between the strands of her hair. They focused on me, then the knife, and widened in horror. Before I knew what she was about, she knocked my arm away and rolled straight into me, landing on the floor at my feet.

I cursed beneath my breath as she hit my legs, making me stumble backwards and giving her just enough room to get her feet underneath her and stand up. Shoving her hair out of her face, she looked around with red, watering eyes, still disoriented from the ether, then yanked the gag from her mouth and spit out the cloth handkerchief.

Dammit. They should've tied her up. Enzo quickly moved between her and the door as I held both hands out in front of me. "No one's gonna hurt you, Nicole." I had no real worry that she would escape. The room was large, and she had a lot of room to get around him, but Enzo was faster on his feet than he appeared.

She blinked hard a few times as she tried to focus on me, her gray eyes still hazy. I stared at this beauty before me, searching for some kind of flaw. With her naturally light skin and pale hair, you'd think she'd be all washed out without a ton of makeup to make her features more interesting, but that wasn't the case with this one. She was a rare one. Young, petite, with just the right amount of curves to keep a man busy. It was easy to see why Mario wanted her for his arm candy, and why he'd kept her identity secret from everyone.

Or so he'd thought.

I slid my knife back into the holster. "See? The knife is gone. I was only going to use it to take the gag off. That's all." I kept my voice low and calm. I didn't care if she was scared. It wouldn't change my plans for her. But if she tried to run right now, I'd have to catch her and force her into submission, and although I would enjoy the fight, it wouldn't really get us off on the right foot.

Enzo took a step to the side and his shoe squeaked on the marble floor. She whipped around, her back stiffening when she saw him standing only a few feet behind her. My eyes dropped to her ass, barely covered by washed-out jean shorts, then down her classic Hollywood legs. I noticed she only had one sandal on, and my eyes went to Enzo.

"Her other shoe is right outside the door," he answered my unspoken question. "It fell off when I was carrying her in. I'll get it as soon as we get this situation under control."

In the split second my attention was diverted, Nicole kicked off her other sandal and surprised me by running barefoot around the couch—and me–toward the French doors that led out to the back deck. She was quick, I had to give her that, but I was more so, and I easily intercepted her before she touched the handle. Ducking down, I threw my shoulder into her waist and used her own momentum to lift her up and over my shoulder.

She hadn't made a sound up until then, other than a small gasp of fear when she saw my knife coming at her. But now, after a moment of shock to find herself ass up, she let loose. "Let me go, you fuckin' prick!"

Enzo's lips twitched as I passed him, heading toward the stairs. "She doesn't look like an Italian girl," he mused. "But she sure as hell sounds like one."

The "she" in question landed a hard kick with the ball of her foot right above my knee and I hefted her higher on my shoulder, then smacked her ass with my free hand, leaving it there when I felt the rounded fullness of her flesh. "Do that again, Nicole, and you'll fucking regret it."

With a screech, she doubled her efforts, kicking and punching and trying to lift herself off my shoulder. Gritting my teeth, I hung on tight to her smooth legs until I made it up the curved stairway, down the hall, and into my room, where I dumped her unceremoniously onto the black comforter of my king-sized bed. Before she could gather herself enough to jump up, I had her held down with the weight of my body and the sharp edge of my knife pressed against the side of her face. "Don't do it," I gritted out. I was fucking exhausted, and in no mood for this shit, which was one of the reasons I'd sent Enzo and Tristan to get her for me. The other reason was that I couldn't have my face anywhere near the scene of her kidnapping. However, that didn't mean I was going to let this bitch go psycho and wreck my lake house.

A bead of blood appeared where the tip of the knife dug into the skin right below her eye. I held her still with my forearm pressed against her chest as I slowly licked it away from my knife, the steel of the blade cold on my tongue compared to her warm skin, the metallic taste of steel mixing with the hint of copper. "Or hell, maybe you should," I goaded. "Scars are sexy."

To my utter disappointment, she stilled, all of the fight draining out of her like air.

Keeping my face right in hers and the knife pressed to her cheek, I told her, "Now. We can play this one of two ways, *amore*. You can keep trying to run and I'll tie you to this fucking bed—which, I gotta be honest, is what I'm hoping for—or you can chill the fuck out and listen to what I have to say. I have a beautiful home. I think you'll enjoy it here if you give it a chance. I also understand you'll have questions, and I'm more than fucking happy to answer them. *If* you can behave like a civilized person. *Comprendere?*"

As she stared up at me, I watched in fascination as her gray eyes turned as cold as the steel of my knife, and I felt her fingers squeeze my shoulders, like she was fighting the urge to try to push me off. I moaned, rolling my hips against hers so she could feel what she was doing to me, ready for any move she would make. But after a moment, her hands dropped to the bed. "I understand," she told me in a firm voice.

I had to admit I was both surprised and intrigued by this little bomb I was straddling. Mario didn't seem the type to hook up with a *donna vivace* like this one. A lively woman. Although I had yet to lay eyes on his fiancée until this week, I'd never known him to like women who actually had a spine. From what I'd seen, he preferred the type who would fall to their knees and suck him off with nothing but a snap of his fingers.

I lessened the pressure of the knife just a bit. "Are we good, *amore?*"

After another brief hesitation, she gave me a small nod. But I wasn't completely convinced by her compliance. Her jaw was clenched so tight that if I was a caring man, I'd be worried she would hurt her teeth. However, I was not that kind of man. Caring meant you were soft. And in the world of the Italian mafia, soft meant dead. Either for you or the one you loved. Nicole was here for one reason and one reason only: revenge. And my chance to win back the respect Mario had fucking taken from me.

Slowly, I sat up and eased my weight off of her, sliding my knife back into its holster before I climbed off the bed and straightened the jacket of my Armani suit. Then I made a show of smoothing the wrinkles from my shirt and pants. Lifting one foot onto the side of the bed, I brushed off the top of my shoe where she'd stepped on it with her dusty flip flop as she got up off the floor. The entire time I fussed with my appearance, I kept her in my peripheral vision, giving her time to decide how she was going to act.

Nicole sat up and quickly looked around the room before her gray eyes landed on the hilt of my knife.

"The only weapons are on me," I answered her unspoken question. Setting my foot back onto the floor, I backed up a few steps and put my arms out to my sides, giving her full view of not only the knife on my side but the Glock I kept on me at all times. "Wanna try it?"

She actually fucking thought about it before she shook her head and averted her eyes. Damn, this woman made me hard.

I dropped my arms, again hiding my disappointment. "Then let's talk. After I tell you why you're here, you can ask me whatever you want, and if at all possible, I'll answer."

"And if not possible?"

"Then you'll just have to trust that I'm only giving you information it's safe for you to know."

I stepped back and gestured toward the two armchairs near the balcony doors. "Please." I didn't worry about her being seen by someone outside. All of the windows on this side of the house faced the lake, and being that my home was perched on the edge of a cliff and my men were on constant lookout for any boats on the water, no one would be able to sneak up on me. "Would you like to sit?"

Still without looking at me, she scooted off the bed and padded barefoot over to the chairs, taking a seat in the one that would put her back to the bedroom door, which only told me she'd led a life where she didn't need to worry about someone stabbing her in the back. Or shooting her from behind. Crossing her shapely legs at the knee, she gripped the arms of the chair and waited.

Taking the seat across from her, I mimicked her pose. After a long, tense moment, she lifted her eyes to me, staring at me like she was trying to place where she'd seen me before.

"Let me start by telling you that you are in my private home. This house is surrounded by twenty acres of a whole lot of nothing but trees and scrub brush and venomous snakes. Out there"—I nodded toward the balcony doors and the gathering darkness on the other side—"is nothing but a three-hundred-foot drop. If you're lucky, you'll hit the water. If not, you'll shatter every bone in your body on the boulders at the base. My men patrol the perimeter of my home at all hours on land and on water. Also, no one knows the location of this home except for me and my men. Not even my own family knows where I sleep. So, for that reason alone, I wouldn't hesitate to kill you if you managed to escape."

"If you could find me," she said.

There was that soft voice again. The one that sent shivers down my spine in the best possible way. A smile teased the corners of my mouth. "Oh, I would find you, Nicole."

Little lines appeared between her perfectly shaped eyebrows as a look of disgust twisted her lush lips. "Why do you keep calling me that? My name is *not* Nicole."

CHAPTER 3
VEDA

I had no idea who this guy was or what he wanted from me, but I would rather he call me anything in the world other than *that* name. Slut. Bitch. Whore. Cunt. Any of those would work. Just not "Nicole." I was still pissed at her.

"Your name is not Nicole," he deadpanned. I could tell by his tone he was only patronizing me. It irked me beyond reason, but I answered anyway. I even managed to keep the sarcasm from my tone.

For the most part.

"No. But if you want her, I'd be more than happy to tell you exactly where to find her." At least I thought I could. I hadn't heard from my sister in two weeks, not until I received that damn wedding invitation in the mail.

"Like the downtown condo where you've lived for the last year? The one your boyfriend...excuse me, your fiancé...pays for?"

I could tell he didn't believe me. And not just from his tone. There was something in his eyes. The cold stare of an alligator right before it locks its teeth around you and pulls you into a death roll. And there was no way for me to prove it to him without getting my purse out of my car that's currently parked in the garage below my sister's place.

Oh, wait! My phone! I leaned forward and slapped my hand over my back pocket before I remembered I'd laid it on the couch beside me before I was so rudely kidnapped. *Dammit.* With a sigh, I sat back again, chewing on my thumbnail. And then I thought of something. "Do you have a Facebook account? Personally, I don't. Social media is bad for the soul. But I'm sure Nicole must have a picture of the two of us somewhere. I could show you who I am."

"And who is that?" he asked without answering my question. "Who are you if not Nicole? The woman marrying Mario Morelli in a few short weeks. Or, at least, the woman who was supposed to marry him."

His voice was low and slightly raspy and way too distracting, but that last sentence caught my attention. "Supposed to? You stole me to stop a wedding?" That made no sense. If my sister was involved with this guy, too, you'd think he would be able to tell us apart.

Also, I now knew the name of my future brother-in-law and I intended to stalk him online as soon as I possibly could.

He didn't answer. Just stared at me with ice-blue eyes so cold they sent a shiver running down my spine.

"Who are *you*?" I demanded. "And why exactly do you want to stop my sister's wedding?"

"Your sister?"

I rolled my eyes before I could think better of it. "Yes. My sister. That's what I've been trying to tell you. You've got the wrong girl."

"That's not possible. Nicole Calbert doesn't have a sister." However, he didn't sound quite so smug now.

"And yet, here I am." I spread my arms out wide and his eyes immediately went to my boobs. I dropped my hands back into my lap and gave him the "are you kidding me right now?" stare us girls have had to perfect over the course of our lives when dealing with men.

He rubbed his jaw as he studied me like I was a piece of abstract art he was trying to figure out, drawing my attention to his strong hands and the gray hairs sprinkled throughout his close-cut beard. Rather than making him look old, it made him look dangerous. Sexy. He wore what looked to be an expensive watch on his wrist. Almost as expensive as the black suit that was exactly tailored to fit his hard body. His sandy brown hair was clipped tight to his head on the sides and back, the top a little bit longer and pushed back from his forehead in natural waves. I noticed there was a bit of gray there, too. On the sides. And from the lines around his eyes, I'd judge him to be in his late thirties. Maybe forty. A man in his prime. He also spoke perfect Italian, yet had absolutely no accent when he switched to English.

And he enjoyed the taste of his victim's blood.

Something sharp and unexpected hit me right in the gut at the thought of this man vying for Nicole's attention, his hard body covering hers the way it had just done mine. His weight pressing her into the mattress. His smell filling her nose and his heat warming her skin. I immediately pushed the images—and whatever the hell it was I was feeling—aside. It was none of my business, what went on between them. And honestly, I really didn't want to know. Or maybe I did.

I sighed loudly. Hell, I don't know. I've hated my sister for so long it was hard to tell if I cared about her anymore. "Look," I told him. "Again, you've got the wrong girl."

"*Again*, that's not possible."

"Why not?"

"Because I don't make mistakes. And neither do my men."

I sighed. There was no use arguing with him. He wasn't going to listen. Instead, I wracked my brain, trying to think of a way I could prove I wasn't my sister. Maybe if I knew more about what was going on, I could somehow force him to understand this was nothing but a case of mistaken identity. "Are you going to tell me why I'm here?"

"Because your boyfriend took someone from me once."

I ignored the first part. For now. "So you're returning the favor?"

"Something like that."

Why did I get the feeling these people weren't in the business of real estate? My heart began to pound as I asked my next question. "Are you going to hurt me?"

"Not right now. Not unless you try to escape."

I studied his face, searching for some sign that he was lying. But he was looking straight at me, his posture alert but relaxed, and he hadn't faltered with his answer. Plus, my instincts told me that this man may be a lot of things, but a liar wasn't one of them. "Okay." I took a deep breath. "How long are you going to keep me here?"

"As long as it takes."

"And what, exactly, are you hoping to accomplish?"

"The answer I gave you will have to be enough. For now."

So the rest falls under "things Veda doesn't need to know." Got it.

"What are you going to do with me while I'm here?"

His head cocked to the side as his eyes raked over me from head to toe and back again. When he was finished, I couldn't fight the urge to actually looked down to make sure my clothes weren't singed from my body by the heat in his gaze. "Whatever I want," he practically growled. "*Nicole.*"

My breath caught in my chest. But I couldn't tell you if it was from fear or...something else.

"However," he continued. "I already told you I wouldn't hurt you while you are a guest in my home. As long as you behave. You have my word on that."

I swallowed hard. "So, you're just going to keep me a prisoner here until you've achieved whatever the hell it is you're trying to achieve."

"That's correct."

I nodded, my eyes straying to the wall of windows on my right. I didn't know what to say. Or think. Honestly, I was still feeling a bit hazy from the wine and whatever they'd drugged me with.

"I think you'll find your stay here quite pleasant," he went on. "The house is large, so you can have some space during the day while I work if you'd like. The views are stunning, especially the sunsets. I have a pool and a hot tub, a media room, and a home gym."

Of course, he did. I'd felt how much he worked out when I was thrown over his hard shoulder. "Where will I be sleeping?"

He was quiet for so long I thought he wasn't going to answer. "You'll be staying in here. With me."

Oh, hell no. That wasn't going to work for me. Until I could convince him otherwise, I was stuck here in this house, but that didn't mean I owed him any favors. "Don't you have a spare room?"

"I have five. But you won't be using any of them."

"Why not?"

"Because your actions up until now have proven to me that I can't trust you."

"That arrangement isn't going to work for me."

"I don't recall giving you a choice."

I disagreed. I always had a choice. However, I didn't see the value of pointing that out to him at this point in time. "And what will be expected of me while I'm here?"

"Only to be ready to go out with me when I need you to."

"Go out where?"

"Wherever I need you to go." At my look, he elaborated. "Dinners. Parties. Things like that."

"But I don't have anything to wear."

His lips twitched, and my breath caught. But the smile I'd expected never formed. "I'll bring someone in to fit you for some clothes."

"If you point me to the nearest computer, I can just order some stuff online." I held his steady gaze even as my heart began to pound at the thought of getting a message to someone, but I should've known it wouldn't be that easy.

"That's not going to happen."

He watched me for a long time as I processed everything he'd just said. I tried not to lose hope, but I had to admit, it was kinda hard.

"Are you hungry?" he finally asked.

I shook my head, refusing to look at him.

He sighed. "What is it, Nicole?"

"I told you. I am *not* Nicole," I gritted through my teeth.

He clenched his jaw, but then he inhaled loudly through his nose and sat forward, resting his elbows on his knees. I tried not to squirm in my seat as the full weight of those blue eyes focused on me. "If your name is not Nicole, then what is it?"

"Veda."

"*Vita?*"

"No. Veda. With a 'd'."

"Veda what?"

"Veda Calbert." Duh.

"Do you have a middle name?"

"Lynn. And before you ask, I'm twenty-two, and I live in an apartment on 8th street on the east side of the city. Nicole is my older sister. But only by a minute. We're twins." Probably way too much information, more than he really needed to know, but if it would get me out of whatever mess my sister had gotten herself into...

He leaned back in his chair, and I could practically feel him digging around in my head to see if I was telling the truth. I jumped when he suddenly called out, "Enzo!"

The guy who'd put the hood over my head and brought me inside appeared in the bedroom doorway a few seconds later. "What do you need?"

Without taking his eyes from me, he told him, "Go into my office and look up Veda Lynn Calbert. Age twenty-two. Lives in an apartment on 8th street on the east side of Austin. And works...?" He trailed off, one eyebrow lifted in question.

"I've been working as an assistant. For my sister. *Nicole*."

He narrowed his eyes at me. "Don't worry about employment. Give him your exact address," he ordered.

I rattled it off to the guy in the bedroom doorway.

"What is this about?" Enzo asked.

"Just do it," he told him. "I'll explain later."

Enzo paused for just a moment before he turned and left the room.

In the minutes that followed, he continued to stare at me. I tried not to squirm. I wasn't a criminal, for god's sake. "What's your name?" I asked him to break the silence.

"Luca," he said quietly.

"Luca what?"

"Just Luca for now."

Uncrossing my legs, I leaned forward and mimicked his pose. "I can't say that it's good to meet you, Luca...all things considered."

He did smile then. A true smile. And as some of the ice in his blue eyes melted away, my heart began to race for a completely different reason.

CHAPTER 4

LUCA

The woman was fucking fearless. I had to admit, I was much more intrigued by her than I'd expected to be.

Leaving her in the bedroom to give her time to accept her new fate, I warned her again that trying to escape was not beneficial to her staying alive, then went downstairs and strode down the hall to my office where I found Enzo staring intensely at the computer monitor.

"What is it?" I asked him.

He didn't move or look up at me. "It's not possible," he said after a moment.

My gut clenched. "What's not fucking possible?"

Finally, he looked at me, and I didn't have to see the monitor to know what he had found. Without a word, I walked around my desk and sat down in my chair as Enzo jumped to his feet.

Two birth certificates were pulled up on the large monitor screen. One for a Nicole Marie Calbert and the other for Veda Lynn Calbert. Born a minute apart on the same day at the same hospital to the same parents.

For a moment, I felt nothing at all. "Why is this the first time I'm seeing this?" I knew the story, but I needed to hear it the fuck again.

"Tito was the one who saw Mario going up to the condo."

Tito was one of my top soldiers. He'd been with me a long time. I trusted him implicitly.

"He knows someone who works in the building, and he was able to disguise himself as a maintenance man and was admitted into the woman's home to make repairs. He engaged her in conversation after seeing the ring on her finger and found out she was, in fact, engaged to Mario. She seems happy enough to blab it to anyone who'll listen. She also told him how she'd been on TV the previous day for an interview. She seemed nervous. Once he gave me the information, I confirmed her name and where she lived, and we watched the interview. Then scoped her place out ourselves, as you know. Birth records were never a part of our investigation for you."

"Maybe they fucking should have been."

Enzo had been with me for a long time. He knew better than to respond to that statement.

I took a few deep breaths, forcing down my temper enough so I could think rationally. Honestly, I didn't really blame

Enzo. With the information we had gotten straight from the horse's mouth, so to speak, there had been no reason to investigate her further. I didn't give a fuck about where she'd gone to grade school or where her first job was. What I cared about was taking her away from Mario. Taking something he loved. Something he would miss. And then blowing off half of her skull right in front of his fucking face and smiling as her brain matter splattered his body.

I could've just killed her on sight. Taken her outside and shot her in the back of the head. But that wasn't enough for me. I wanted to see the fear in his eyes. Wanted to watch him grieve for her. Wanted to tear his fucking heart from his chest for choosing his life over loyalty to the family. Over loyalty to *me*. Then, and only then, would I put him out of his misery.

My pulse sped up again and blood began to pound in my ears as my hands clenched into fists on the desk. I wanted to hit something. But going off half-cocked would not fix this problem. I'd take out my anger on the punching bag in my gym later.

"What should we do with the woman?"

I sat back in my chair. There was really nothing to think about. She knew who we were. She'd seen our faces. She knew I lived on a lake. Even if I were to let her go, that was too much information. Anyone with half a brain would figure out who had taken her. And my home, the only safe place I had in this city, would be found not long after. If I was lucky, it would be the police who found me, and not Mario or the Cartel.

And if my home was infiltrated, and I happened to live through all of that, I would become a liability to the family. In jail or on the run, my father would take me out. I didn't take it personally. It was business. He couldn't be seen as weak in any way. Not even for his own son. Luigi —my father—was the main boss. It was a position he'd hung onto for the past forty-three years, and nothing as insignificant as myself would remove him from being head of the family.

So I couldn't just let her go. And that left me with only one option.

But then something else came to me. Until we found out where her sister was, Veda was the only possible card I held against Mario. At least until I found the real Nicole. They looked enough alike he wouldn't know the difference unless he was close to her. And if I had my way, he would never get within six feet of her. My blood boiled at the thought of my brother anywhere near Veda. "She stays here. For now."

"What about the plan?"

"The plan stays the same until we find out where the actual Nicole Calbert is and how she slipped under our radar. I also need to know if Mario has been with her since Veda came here."

"Of course."

"Where is Tristan?"

"He's on his way back."

I got up from the desk and started walking toward the door. "Fill him in when he gets here, then I want the both of you to personally find Nicole Calbert. This information doesn't go any further than the three of us."

"Yes, sir."

I strode down the hallway toward my home gym, needing to work out some of this anger before I saw Veda again.

How could this have happened? How the hell could I have fucked things up to this extent?

Restlessly, I clenched my fists and released them again, aching to hit something. But then I forced myself to relax and took a deep breath. There was no way I could have known there were twins. I put my best guys on this shit. Not one of them had discovered that there were two girls who looked exactly the same. One engaged to Mario, and one who was not. And we'd had to move in fast. It was a mistake anyone could have made.

However, my father would not see it that way.

When I got to the gym, I stripped down, grabbed a pair of shorts I kept there for occasions such as this, and then I went straight to the punching bag. I've been training in mixed martial arts since I was four, and I knew how to hit a bag. But this right here, right now, this was all about taking out my anger at myself.

Thirty minutes later, when Veda wandered down and found me there, my knuckles were bruised and my knees and the tops of my shins and feet were red. Sweat dripped down my face, my breathing was ragged, and I was still pissed off.

"What did you find out?" she asked me from the doorway, a glint of hope in her expression.

I watched her reflection in the wall of mirrors, but I didn't turn around. "You're supposed to be waiting in my room." Thinking she didn't have my full attention, I didn't miss the way her eyes traveled down my body, lingering at my thighs and ass before they wandered over my back and arms. But she was smart enough not to come any closer.

Looking at her, standing there in what little she was wearing, my blood roared so loud in my ears I barely heard what she'd said, my body screaming for release, but not from the bag. "You have a sister," was the only response I gave her.

"Uh, yeah, that's what I've been telling you," she answered.

I glared at her over my shoulder, turned, and punched the bag again, but the aggression behind it was less than it had been. A part of me had felt relief when I saw her standing there in the doorway, and I admitted to myself I was glad she wasn't her sister. But I couldn't admit more, no matter how much my body tried to tell me. Not yet. Not until I knew we didn't need her.

"So, what now?" she asked me.

"Nothing changes," I told her. Grabbing a towel from the bench, I wiped off my face, my anger at myself renewed. How fucked up was I, lusting after some girl when the only thing I should be thinking about was finding her sister and carrying out my plan.

Shock swept over her face. "What do you mean, nothing changes?"

"Just what I said," I gritted out. I was swiftly growing tired of her questions. I needed to be alone to think.

"What the fuck do you mean?" she repeated, her voice rising. "I'm not the right person."

"It doesn't matter," I said as I wiped the sweat from my chest.

She took a few steps into the room, and I could clearly see the panic in her eyes. "But you can just let me go now."

I lowered the towel and looked straight at her. "No, Veda, I can't."

As the meaning of my words sank in, she swayed on her feet. "You're going to kill me," she whispered. "But I don't know anything. I don't know where this house is. I don't even know who you are! Not really..."

She was scared, and she had a right to be. She should be fucking terrified, because that's exactly what I should do. But this woman intrigued me, and despite the way she disobeyed everything I told her to do, I found I liked having her near me. "That's not what I said," I told her.

She walked on stiff legs over to the wall of mirrors and leaned her back against it before her knees gave out and she sank down to the floor. "Then what?" she asked. "I'm your prisoner forever?"

"I didn't say that, either," I told her.

She looked up at me then. "What exactly *are* you saying, Luca?"

That was a good fucking question, wasn't it. I wrapped the towel around the back of my neck and grabbed a water bottle out of the small fridge in the corner. "I need to find your sister before I decide what I'm going to do with you," I told her.

"And if you find her?" she asked in a quiet voice.

"Then you won't be needed anymore." At least not for my plans of revenge.

But somewhere in the red haze of my anger, another plan began to form. One where I wouldn't have to give up this beauty I'd only just found, if only I could find her sister. Either way, there was no chance in hell Veda was ever going back to what she'd known before. The only life she would have now was one with me in it, however long that would be. My instincts told me she belonged here. With me. I wasn't sure yet exactly why that was, but I always followed my instincts.

Well, except once. And there was no fucking way that would happen again.

Maybe she would take the place of her sister and help me rip Mario's heart from his chest the way he had mine. Maybe she'd end up being one of my best spies. Maybe she was just going to be *mine*. I didn't know, and I didn't fucking care. I just knew she wasn't leaving.

"And if you don't find her?" she said, as if she'd read my mind.

"Then perhaps you and I can come to some sort of agreement."

"Like, what kind of agreement?" she asked, looking up at me in confusion.

"The kind that will make you useful to me, which means I will keep you alive."

She mulled that over for a moment. "So, you just expect me to hang out here and wait."

"Yes," I told her. "That's exactly what I expect you to do." I paused, took a sip of my water, and eyed her over the bottle. "If you're not the praying type, Veda, now would probably be a good time to take that up."

She laughed, but it was an ugly sound. "I have a life. I have people who will miss me. They'll report me missing."

"I'll take care of it."

She stared at me like I'd lost my mind. "I'm a fucking human being! You can't just kidnap me like this and expect me to do whatever the hell you say."

"I can. And I did. And you will."

Fire warmed her gray eyes. "Or what? You'll kill me?" She pushed herself up from the floor, and I could practically see her entire body vibrating with her anger. It was fucking beautiful. A rage that rivaled my own. "Go ahead," she spit the words at me. "Death would be preferable to staying here with you and being your puppet."

God, she was stunning. And infuriating. My own men didn't mouth off to me the way this woman did. I crossed the room and stood directly in front of her before she had time to run. Grabbing her jaw, I forced her to look at me. "Keep mouthing off to me, Veda. I dare you."

Taking a step back, she jerked her chin from my grasp, then slapped me across the face. Hard.

A deadly calm came over me. Slowly, I turned my head back around until our gazes clashed. Whatever she saw there wiped the rebellious look from her face. A heartbeat passed. Then another...

Lurching to the left, she tried to run. But I was expecting it and caught her around the waist, lifting her off the floor and pulling her back against my chest. Her ass felt good against my cock, and it swiftly hardened in response. My free hand wrapped around her throat, cutting off most of her air supply. Veda clawed at my forearm, leaving bloody scratches in my skin, but I barely felt it. Putting my mouth right next to her ear, I said, "You want to die? Is that what you really want, Veda?"

She struggled to speak, and I tightened my hold.

"Because I can help you with that, *amore*."

In the mirror, I could see her eyes, too large for her face as they widened in terror, and her lips were beginning to turn blue. Her struggles became desperate.

"Do not fucking hit me again," I growled. "Or I won't be so nice next time." I opened my arms, and she fell to her hands and knees on the floor, coughing and gagging and clawing at her throat.

When she finally managed a rasping breath, I crouched down behind her, sitting on the balls of my feet, and pulled her up against me again. She tried to call out, as though someone would help her, her eyes red and filled with tears as she watched our reflection in the mirror. "Shhh," I told her, gently moving her hair from her face. She smelled like her shampoo and whatever lotion she used, and she was still shaking. But not from anger this time.

Something caught in my chest, and I held her close. I didn't like her being afraid of me. However, I also couldn't have her acting out against me the way she just had.

"Let me go," she whispered, her voice hoarse.

"I can't," I whispered back. *I need you.*

Something wet hit my arms, and I realized she was crying. "I can't," I told her again, louder this time, not knowing who I was trying to convince. Veda...or myself.

Little did I know how true that statement would become, but not at all for the reasons I'd thought.

CHAPTER 5

VEDA

I walked back to Luca's room with him. Not that I had a choice.

Shortly after he tried to—I gingerly touched my neck—fucking *strangle* me in the workout room, he breathed a deep sigh and helped me to my feet, his hands gentle, yet still trembling with anger as he guided me from the room.

My throat ached and tears dampened my cheeks and my head felt like it was in a fog. I've never had anyone hurt me like that, and I wasn't sure how to process it. As we walked through the house, my eyes darted back and forth, looking for the other guy who'd brought me here, but luckily, he was nowhere to be found. I didn't want anyone to see me like this.

Luca shut the door behind us when we reached his room. "I need a shower," he told me. "And you're getting one, too."

"I don't need a shower." It hurt to talk. My voice sounded like only half of my vocal cords were working, and I wondered if he'd permanently damaged them.

"I don't remember asking you," he said.

For once, I managed to keep my mouth shut. A shower wouldn't be the worst thing in the world. What bothered me about it was that I had to share it with him.

Grabbing some stuff out of the large dresser near the bathroom door, Luca took my hand and pulled me along with him to the bathroom, my hopes for having any semblance of privacy shattered.

Surrounded by three walls of clear glass, there was a walk-in entrance on one end of the shower. It took up most of one wall and was long enough to fit six people inside. Two shower heads and two sets of temperature control levers came out of the wall. A stone bench big enough for two sat below them. Across from the shower was a large white bathtub. An actual fucking chandelier hung above it, and the entire wall behind it was one large window that looked out over the lake. The toilet was in its own room near a dressing table. *Thank god for small favors.* The marble floors were warm beneath my bare feet.

"Get undressed," he ordered.

"No." The word left my mouth before I could stop it. A jolt of fear shot through me as I waited for his reaction.

But he only clenched his jaw as he stared at me. Stepping into me, he ran his fingers through a few strands of my hair where it fell over my left shoulder. He was so close I could smell the sweat on his hard body and could feel the heat radiating from him. I swayed toward him, inexplicably drawn to that heat. And it was only then I realized how cold I was.

"The water will feel good, Veda."

"Are you going to rape me?" I wouldn't be able to stop him. But somehow, I thought that if I knew what he was about to do I could deal with it. I just needed to know what to expect, was all.

He became very still, and I could feel his gaze, heavy on my face as he searched for something in my expression. "No," he finally said, and I sensed he was somehow affronted. "No. I wouldn't do that."

"So, you only...assault women...with your hands...and not...with your dick." *Shut up, Veda! For fuck's sake. He's going to kill you.*

But to my surprise, his fingers moved from my hair to my face. Gently, he lifted my chin with one finger. And when I got up the nerve to look at him, there was a twinge of regret darkening his blue eyes. "I reacted before I thought about what I was doing. But if you're waiting for an apology, *amore,* you'll be waiting a long time. You need to understand who you're dealing with here. I'm not some green boy-child who you can control with a bat of your long eyelashes. I am a grown man. I've lived a hard life. And I'm still alive because I don't let anyone get away with shit like what you just pulled. And *you* will only stay that way if you learn to control that bitch of a temper of yours."

His hand slid down to the front of my throat and I bit back a wince as he probed the sensitive skin. But honestly, it frightened me more than it hurt.

"Now get undressed," he repeated when he was satisfied with whatever he was doing, his tone cold and hard. Walking around me, he dropped his shorts and boxer briefs to the floor and got into the shower. Turning on the water, he let it run over his hand until steam began to rise, then he adjusted the temperature. "Now, Veda."

I tore my eyes from the sleek lines of his body as he moved under the water and turned around to wet his hair, but not before the image was seared into my mind.

Luca was long and lean, but tall enough and muscular enough to make me feel tiny in comparison. And after seeing him go after that punching bag, I could see why. His back was broad, his ass was tight, and his legs and arms were powerful. There was nothing about this man that wasn't completely masculine.

It was really too bad he was such an asshole.

"Veda."

His tone told me I'd put this off as long as I would be allowed. My eyes shot to the bathroom door. I could make a run for it. I still didn't have my shoes, but it wouldn't be the first time I took my chances with fire ants and cactus. I just had to make it to the road. Or into the lake. I was an excellent swimmer. Then I could find the closest house and beg for help. He had to have neighbors. We weren't that far out of the city.

Attuned to his every movement, I noticed right away when he stopped washing himself. Glancing over my shoulder, I found him watching me, both palms against the glass, steam rising around him, caressing his skin like a lover. "If you think I won't chase you because I'm naked and wet, you're wrong. However, if you still want to run, *do it.*"

It was a dare. One I would be stupid to take. With shaking hands, I took off my T-shirt and bra and dropped my shorts and panties to the floor. Covering myself with my hands and arms as best I could, I walked into the shower, keeping my eyes on my bare feet.

"Come here, *amore.*"

Swallowing hard, I inched my way under the water as Luca moved out of the way. I wasn't sure exactly what to expect, but it definitely wasn't what happened.

He didn't scold me for covering up or force me to drop my arms. Instead, he carefully guided me back beneath the spray, urging me to tilt my head back with a tight grip on my long hair. When all of the strands were wet, he lathered it up with shampoo, and I had to fight back a moan as his long fingers massaged my scalp with just the right pressure.

Once my hair was clean and rinsed, he soaped up the shower pouf and stepped behind me to wash my back. I stiffened and tried to turn around, but he kept one hand on my bare shoulder, holding me still as he scrubbed my skin in slow circles. It felt so good that I finally just dropped my chin and let him do it. When I'd relaxed somewhat, he moved down to my ass and legs.

I stood there like a child and let him wash me, my mind devoid of thought except for how good it felt to let someone take care of me for a change. His movements were straightforward and functional, and other than the fact that he was touching me more intimately than anyone had in a long, long time, he kept the whole thing surprisingly business-like.

Something lazy and warm began to heat my insides. It started low in my belly and twisted through my body until my skin was so sensitive the glide of the soapy pouf left a trail of fire in its wake so hot the water had to cool me down. I knew it was fucked up. How could I feel anything but anger after what he'd just done to me in the gym?

And yet, I did.

"Turn around."

My head snapped up at the huskiness of his voice, and I froze. Standing beneath the water with him behind me, it took me a moment to understand that despite his tone, he was giving me the choice to do as he said. I had no doubt at all that if I didn't obey him, he would get frustrated and either force me to turn around or he'd just walk around me and do what he wanted to anyway, but still, he gave me the illusion of a choice.

I turned around.

The water was now at my back, and Luca reached around me to wet the pouf and add more soap. As I stood with my arms covering my breasts, he gently washed my face and neck, then my shoulders and arms. There, he stopped and waited, his eyes on my face.

I stared at him for a long time, knowing this was the first step of my surrender. Then I dropped my arms.

He studied me a moment longer, then he ran the pouf down my torso, between my breasts, from my chest to my stomach. I watched him as his eyes followed the trail he made. Watched as his nostrils flared and his breath came louder and faster. His cock, already half hard, swelled to an impressive size.

Apparently, he wasn't as all business as I'd thought. And I wasn't sure how that made me feel. I mean, physically? Sure. But emotionally...no.

Squatting down in front of me, he washed my stomach, legs, feet—and everything in between—slowly and methodically. And when he straightened to his full height and his eyes met mine again, something changed within them. There was knowledge there now that hadn't been there before. Knowledge of me. And I supposed he could probably say the same of mine. I stared at his chest, spotting a few gray hairs in the light dusting of golden brown. I had to forcibly keep my eyes from wandering down his hard stomach to that sexy "V" at his hips, and lower...

He visibly swallowed. "There's a towel right there you can use. And I brought you a clean shirt and shorts you can sleep in."

I looked in the direction he'd tilted his head and found the towel rack. Turning my back to him, I rinsed off, then covered myself again and left him to finish his shower, not quite knowing how not to be awkward as I dried off and put on the things he'd grabbed for me to wear. The clothes were too big for the most part, though a little less so around my hips, but they were soft and comfy, and the shorts had a drawstring so they didn't fall down.

As I got dressed, everything that had happened since I'd gotten here spun round and round in my head. This man I'd so casually taken a shower with had just kidnapped me. Strangled me for slapping him. And then washed it all away without ever actually touching anything with his hands but my hair. He hadn't made any crude remarks. Hadn't made me feel ashamed. It wasn't what I'd expected. He'd told me he wouldn't sexually assault me, and I'd believed him, but I also thought...

Well, I didn't know what I'd thought would happen. I just figured something unsavory would.

"Go ahead and get into bed, Veda. It's late, and I'm tired."

I made a stop in the water closet—I assumed I didn't need permission to pee—washed my hands, and walked into the bedroom. But I didn't go to the bed as ordered, even though I was exhausted. My nerves were still too keyed up. Instead, I wandered over to the patio door, opened it, and went outside into the humid night air. There were two padded chairs on the balcony, and I sat in one. As I waited for whatever was to come next, I stared out into the night, listening to the water gently lap at the rocks down below. An owl hooted somewhere to my left, and then all was quiet again.

My head hurt, and I tried not to think. But I couldn't stop my mind from spinning. What the hell was going to happen to me now? Where the fuck was Nicole? Did anyone miss me yet? I tried to remember if I'd talked to anyone before I'd gone over to my sister's. If I'd made plans with Sammy. But the truth was I spent so much time doing Nicole's bidding I didn't have a lot of time for a social life.

A painful sob burst from me before I could stop it, and I slapped a hand over my mouth. Oh, god. No one would be looking for me. At least not right away. And by the time someone did notice I hadn't been around, I could be buried in this guy's backyard or "swimming with the fishes."

I laughed out loud even as more tears streamed down my cheeks. Do mob dudes actually talk like that?

The patio door opened behind me, and Luca appeared wearing nothing but some loose pajama bottoms, the same gray as my shorts. He had a teacup in his hand.

I quickly wiped my face and put my hands demurely in my lap.

His eyes went from my face to my hands. He frowned, but didn't question me. "Here." He handed it to me. "It's hot, so be careful."

"What is it?"

"Green tea with honey. It'll help your throat."

Maybe it was honey. Maybe it was poison. Either way, I took the cup from him and took a sip, not sure which one I hoped it was. He was right. It felt good going down. When I didn't start cramping up or spitting blood, I swallowed a sigh of relief and drank some more. Guess I still wanted to live. Even as a prisoner.

When he was satisfied I'd had enough, Luca sat down beside me. He was quiet for a long time. Then he said, "Let's make a deal, you and I."

I sipped my tea and waited for him to go on.

"Tomorrow, we'll start looking for your sister. All I ask is that you hang tight here until we find her. That you don't try to run. And that you don't fight me, especially not in front of my men. If you can do that, life will be a lot easier for the both of us." He looked over at me. "A few days, Veda. That's all I ask."

I lowered my cup. It might be horribly selfish of me, or maybe I was just in survival mode, but the fact that my sister was soon going to take my place stirred no emotion inside of me.

"And when those few days are up, I'll either be dead or I'll have to pretend to be my sister for as long as you need me, which will only gain me a little time until you *don't* need me anymore."

He didn't respond, but that was the only reason he could be keeping me here like this. I couldn't think of anything else. Either way, my life was in this man's hands.

CHAPTER 6
LUCA

I held Veda close to me throughout the night. I told her it was because I didn't trust her, but that wasn't the reason why. Even if I was asleep, there was no way she would escape me. I had cameras and silent alarms everywhere. So many that the only person allowed in my house at night was Enzo, and I texted him when I was about to go to sleep so he would know the house was fully activated. He had the codes if he needed to move around. Tristan stayed in a guest house on my property, as did the rest of my men when I needed them here. If not, they went home to their families.

It wasn't that I trusted Enzo more. I'd known Tristan just as long. We'd fucked girls together...had family meals together...killed together...

Enzo had just been the (not so) lucky one to call the right side of the coin. When he got tired of it, I'd change the codes and switch to Tristan. The less people that knew them, the safer it was for all involved.

With Veda's back against my front and her perfect ass cradled by my hips, it took her a long time to relax against me and fall asleep, her chest rising and falling with deep, slow breaths and her mouth slightly parted in sleep. Rolling onto my back, I touched the bottom of the lamp on the nightstand until the bed was lit with a soft glow. Slowly, so as not to wake her, I pulled her blonde hair away from her throat.

"I'm asking for a truce."

Those were the words I'd given her, and I was surprised to realize now that she was so calm and quiet I didn't really mean them. I enjoyed the fire in this woman.

Her pale skin was still a little red where my hand had cut off her breath, but no bruising as of yet. I don't know why this proof of my violent nature was bothering me so much I couldn't find sleep myself. I'd done much worse things to much more innocent people. But for some reason, seeing the evidence of my hands rough on her skin—pain I'd inflicted myself—hit me right in the gut.

Rolling back over, I shut off the lamp. But I didn't sleep. Not for a long time.

What the fuck was it about her that affected me so much? I barely knew her. Expelling a long breath, I tried to find a comfortable position.

If I was smart, I'd give her over to Tristan and have him keep her in the guest house out of my sight. That had been my original plan, until she'd tried to run. Once she did that, I had no choice but to hunt her. I'd instinctively brought her up to my room, and I'd had this inexplicable need to keep her near me ever since. Hell, I even forced her into the shower with me. For what? Some false sense of intimacy?

It made no sense. It's not like I was starving for female company. I had multiple women ready to drop everything for me—including their panties—whenever I snapped my fingers.

If my father heard about this, he'd tell me immediately I was too distracted by her. That history was repeating itself. But that's not what this was. Veda was a fighter, that's all. And I couldn't take the chance she would get away from me before I had the chance to find out where the real Nicole was. Just in case what I suspected was true, and I ended up needing her after all.

She whimpered in her sleep, as though she sensed how obsessed my thoughts were with her, and I curled my body around hers, wrapping her tight in my arms. I smelled my shampoo in her hair, and once again her ass cradled my cock like that was the only place it was meant to be. She fit against me perfectly, and after a moment, she settled down.

I still didn't sleep. Instead, I enjoyed the feel of her against me while I remembered the vision of her naked and wet in my shower. It had taken everything in my power to honor my promise not to touch her. And I'd almost kept it. But in the end, I couldn't keep myself from feeling the heavy strands of her hair in my hands. Or brushing her soft skin with the very tips of my fingers as I washed her luscious body.

I thought briefly of getting back in there alone and taking care of the painful hard on I was going to have all night, but in the end, I couldn't bring myself to leave her. It was a sweet kind of torture, keeping her so close without allowing myself to have her, and I readily admitted I was a masochist. But this burgeoning obsession I had with this woman could *not* go any farther. I didn't care if my dick turned purple and fell off. The only woman I'd ever allowed myself to care about had been killed as she rode my cock. If I allowed myself to grow attached to Veda, she was sure to meet a similar fate. Like any mafia man worth his salt, I had too many enemies.

Somewhere in the early morning hours, I fell asleep, visions of Veda with a bullet hole between her gray eyes dancing around in my head.

THE NEXT MORNING, I woke up to find Veda wasn't beside me. My heart pounding in my throat, I bolted out of bed and was halfway to the door when I heard the water come on in the bathroom sink. I immediately changed direction, opening the door without knocking.

Veda stood in front of the sink, brushing her teeth.

With *my* fucking toothbrush.

She froze for a few seconds when she saw me standing in the doorway, but when I said nothing, she resumed what she was doing, her eyes never leaving me in the mirror.

Crossing my arms over my bare chest in an attempt to hide the rapid rise and fall of my breathing, I leaned casually against the doorframe, watching her. As I waited for the panic to die off, I nearly managed to convince myself I was only reacting this way because Veda was my ace in the hole, and not because I gave a fuck that she could've found a way out despite all of my precautions. Or worse, gotten shot down by my men patrolling the grounds.

The image of her body on the ground with her limbs twisted beneath her at odd angles, her clothes blood-soaked, and her bright eyes dulled by death flashed through my mind, overtaking the swiftly fading memories of my dreams.

Something I hadn't felt in a long time roared through my blood, and I shook the image away. But I made a mental note to lighten the patrols around my home to the bare minimum. Just for now.

Veda spit into the sink, then rinsed out my toothbrush and put it back into the holder. Pulling her hair away from her face, she cupped one hand, using it to catch the water and rinse out her mouth.

I stared at her reflection in the mirror. More specifically, at the developing bruises marring the pale skin of her throat. It bothered me much more than it should. This woman meant nothing to me. So why did I feel like shit for teaching her a lesson she desperately needed to learn?

"Are you just going to stand there creeping on me all day, or did you need to use the bathroom?"

Her voice was still raspy, but not as bad as it had been last night. "I'm sorry about your throat," I told her, surprising myself.

Veda said nothing as she started opening drawers. When she found what she was looking for—my hairbrush—she began to brush the knots out of her hair with quick, jerky movements.

I pushed myself off the doorframe and took a step into the room. "Stop."

"There's nothing else here for me to use," she protested.

Taking the hairbrush from her hand, I pointed at the chair in front of the dressing table. "Sit." When she looked like she was about to argue with me, I raised both eyebrows, and with a wary look in her eyes, she did as I told her.

Her hair was beautiful. A natural wheat blonde, slightly darker toward her scalp and lighter on the ends. I took a section in one hand and began to brush out the knots, starting at the bottom. And as I brushed, I talked. "Today, I'm going to find out where your sister is. I don't foresee that I'll have to leave the house, I should be able to do what I need to do from my office here. But if I do, I'll leave either Enzo or Tristan here with you for your protection." I finished the section of hair I was working on and started on the next, ignoring the mutinous look she was giving me, but very glad to see a good night's sleep had given her back a bit of her spunk. "You may do whatever you'd like, as long as you stay inside the house. You're not to so much as step outside. And only keep to the balconies that overlook the lake if you need some fresh air." My main concern was that she didn't talk to anyone other than the three of us who knew her real identity. Not until I could straighten out this mess I'd made.

"So I can snoop through your stuff and try on all of your clothes?"

She definitely hadn't lost her fight after our little skirmish the night before, and I was glad to see it. However, I fought to keep my expression stern as I told her, "If you'd like. Anything that's worth any real value to me is either in my safe or in my head. And as far as my clothes go, just hang them back up when you're done." I had to admit, I liked the thought of her wearing my things, of knowing the next time I put them on that the material that was touching my skin had also touched hers.

I glanced up to find her watching me in the mirror with a bemused expression. "You seem surprised by my answer."

"I am," she admitted. "I was half expecting you to finish the job you started last night because I'm being a smartass."

I said nothing else until I finished brushing her hair. Then I left her where she was and put my brush back in the drawer over by the sink. "I don't consider myself a violent man, Veda." Turning back to her, I half sat on the sink, not trusting myself to get closer. "But I grew up in a violent world. And I've learned to do what I need to do to survive."

She watched me in the mirror but didn't turn around. "By what I've seen of you so far, I'd have to say I don't agree with that assessment of yourself."

"Fair enough," I told her after a moment. The reason she was here—or her sister, if we managed to find her—was very important to me. If everything went as planned, I would not only have the respect of my father, but I would also once again secure my position in the family. I needed to win Veda over to my side, or at least make sure she would do what I needed her to do, just in case I needed her. If I fucked this up...

No. I wasn't even going to consider that option. I wouldn't fail.

I couldn't.

"Are you in the mafia? Is that what this is?"

Her question pulled me from my thoughts. "I belong to *cosa nostra*. My family is well-known in the society."

"So that's a yes? Italian, right?"

I gave her a nod. Maybe if she knew exactly who she was dealing with, it would help her remember her manners.

Veda broke eye contact in the mirror and her chin dropped to her chest. I wished I could see her face, but that hair I loved so much hid her from me. I let her think about that while I brushed my teeth and took a piss. When I returned to the sink to wet my hair and push it back off my face, she was still in the same position she'd been in when I'd left. "What is it?" I asked her.

But she just shook her head.

Frowning, I approached her. "Veda?" I touched the back of her head, unable to keep my hands from the softness of her hair.

"Please, just leave me alone," she told me, her throat thick with tears.

Something heavy landed in the center of my chest as I ran my fingers through the silky strands. "Come on now. Dealing with you has been like trying to control a spitting viper since you opened your eyes and found yourself on my couch. What is all this?"

She sniffed, wiping at her face before she lifted her head, but her eyes were red and shiny with tears when she whispered. "I'm going to die."

Ah. That. "I won't let that happen." As soon as the words were out of my mouth, I winced. I had a lot of power in the organization, but I was not my father. I didn't have the final say. I could plead her case, but if the decision was made to take her out, there would be nothing I could do about it.

If I was smart, I would even do it myself before anyone caught wind of her existence.

I dropped my hand from her hair. This woman and her tears were making me weak. Clouding my judgement. And I'd only just met her.

Fuck her and her sad eyes. I allowed myself to get distracted over a woman once.

It would not happen again.

CHAPTER 7
VEDA

He left me sitting in the bathroom. Before walking out, he grumbled something about helping myself to whatever I could find to wear until he could get me some clothes. So I guess he wasn't kidding about feeling free to play in his closet.

I'm really going to die.

The thought hit me out of nowhere, and I took a shuddering breath. There was no other outcome I could see happening in this scenario. Once Luca had my sister, I would be nothing but a risk to his identity and location. Someone who saw too much. Knows too much. He would have to kill me. He would have no other choice. Not only could I go to the police, I would be bait for his enemies—and a man like him would have many—to torture into giving up details about Luca. And I highly doubted they would treat me as a "guest" in their home the way Luca did, as far as that went anyway. I knew I could have it much worse.

As soon as he'd confirmed my suspicions about who he was and what he did for a living, the truth had hit me like I'd just been slapped in the face with a fish.

There's no way I'm getting out of this alive.

I don't know how long I sat there trying to wrap my mind around this realization. I heard Luca get dressed and leave the bedroom, but not before he called someone and asked them to bring me some coffee and food. Reluctant to encourage the passing of time, I stayed frozen where I was until I heard a knock just before the door opened.

"Hello? Miss Calbert?" a female voice called out.

Rising from the chair, I shuffled to the bedroom to find an older woman with short, salt and pepper hair setting a tray on the small table by the patio doors. She was wearing dark slacks, comfortable shoes, and a mint green, short-sleeved pullover top.

When the things on the tray were arranged to her liking, she stood and turned toward me, a pleasant smile on her round face. Deep lines were carved around her eyes and mouth. It lit up her entire face. "Hi!" she said brightly. Striding toward me, she put out her hand. "I'm Lisa. I work for Mr. Morelli."

I took her hand more out of habit than anything else. "Veda." I cocked my head to the side. "So that's his full name?"

She held my hand as a look of surprise crossed her face. "Um, well, I hope so. Because that's what I've been calling him for six years." Then she smiled and released my hand. "I brought you some coffee with sugar and cream on the side since I wasn't sure how you liked it. Or do you prefer tea?" When I shook my head, she continued. "I also brought you a bagel and some cream cheese and jelly."

"I'm not much of a breakfast eater," I told her.

"Me, either," she responded. "But we'll just leave this here in case you get hungry."

It was only then that her eyes dropped to the bruises on my neck. Her face tight with concern, she started to lift her hand toward me, but then seemed to remember where she was and who I was and let it fall back down to her side. "What the hell happened? Are you okay?"

Walking around her, I sat down on one of the chairs and started fixing my coffee. "I slapped your boss across the face."

"No, you did not," she burst out, both hands flying up to cover her mouth. Then she joined me at the table, sitting in the other chair, her lips pressed tight and her eyes flashing. "That still gave him no right to do that to you."

I was surprised she sat down with me, but honestly, I was starved for any company other than Luca's. I wasn't stupid, though. She worked for the mob. And that meant she was completely loyal to them. Not me. I didn't expect her to help me, but it was nice to have another woman to talk to. And maybe I could get some kind of information out of her as to who I was dealing with here. "I assume you know him well."

"Mr. Morelli?" She shrugged. "I know him as well as anyone could, I guess. He gives me free rein around his house, and honestly doesn't care if I use his pool during my break. I can watch TV while I'm fixing dinner. FaceTime with my mom. Whatever. But otherwise, he keeps things pretty business-like."

"You know he's monitoring everything you say and do here, right?" I watched her over the rim of my cup as I took a sip of my coffee. It was still hot, and really good.

"Pfft." She rolled her eyes and waved her hand in the air. "Of course. But that's fine. If he wants to listen in to my mom talking about her hemorrhoids, that's his prerogative."

I almost spit out my coffee. Carefully, I swallowed and then started coughing as Lisa grinned at me.

"It's true, though. That's about as exciting as our conversations get."

"Should you even be talking to me?" Immediately, I threw up one hand so she didn't get the wrong idea. "I mean, won't you get in trouble?"

Lisa shrugged. "I don't know. Mr. Morelli hasn't ever kidnapped anyone before." Before I could expound on the look of disbelief that had to be written all over my face, she nodded. "Yeah. I know he took you against your will. And all I'm going to tell you is unless you have a death wish, you won't try to escape, because you won't make it. And as for our talking, I'm sure he'll let me know if he doesn't want me doing it."

"Aren't you scared of him?" I asked. Her blasé attitude about it all both fascinated me and pissed me off.

"I don't give him a reason to scare me," she answered in a serious tone. "I do as he tells me to do without question, and he pays me some serious money to work in his home."

"Do you live here or somewhere else?"

"Oh no, I live in my own house about forty-five minutes away with my husband and our dog."

The look on my face must've told her I found that hard to believe, for she elaborated. "We both had to sign an NDA in order for me to work here. And Mr. Morelli interviewed us both himself and did background checks." She paused. "Actually, it was a little more intense than that. He knows everything there is to know about us, along with our friends and our families."

I understood then. She would never rat him out because he would go after people she cared about. "You don't worry about his enemies coming after you? Breaking into your house?"

She looked down at her hands, linked together on her lap. "I do." Then she looked back up at me. "But I'm treated well here. He's generous with time off. And with my paycheck. Mr. Morelli makes my life much easier in a lot of ways, and to me it's worth the risk because I know he'll take every precaution to make sure nothing happens to us."

Money. Of course. It's what makes the world go round these days.

"Would you like a tour of the house after you get dressed?"

I'd already wandered around a bit by myself the night before. That's how I'd found Luca in the gym, beating the shit out of that punching bag. But it would be better than staying cooped up in here alone. And maybe I could get some more information out of Lisa. Something that would help me either get out of here, or at the very least, live through this experience. "Sure. That would be nice. Thanks."

She got up. "Take your time finishing your coffee. When you're ready, just come find me in the kitchen. It's down the stairs, across the great room, and through the doorway to your right."

"I'll find you."

Lisa smiled. "See you in a bit." Then she let herself out of the room.

After she was gone, I took another shower, wanting to wash Luca's smell off of me after sleeping next to him in his bed all night. Even with the bathroom door locked, I jumped at every little noise—real or imagined—thinking it was him barging in. Something as insignificant as a lock wouldn't keep him out. I knew this in my gut. But I locked that damned door anyway. If nothing else, it would let him know I preferred to be alone.

This time I was able to appreciate the luxury of steaming hot water hitting the back of my neck and shoulders with just enough pressure, the stunning view of the lake from the window across from me on the far side of the bathtub, and the warmth of the floors and towels when I got out. Much as I would've liked to linger under the spray and imagine I was anywhere but where I was, I didn't dare take too long. It didn't matter to me that Luca had already seen everything there was to see of my body. Last night I was hurt, both physically and emotionally, and running on my instinct to survive. Today, I was still running on that instinct, and it didn't include providing a peep show for my kidnapper.

Five minutes later, I was dressed in another plain black T-shirt and a pair of gray cotton gym shorts I'd found in one of Luca's drawers. My hair wet and my feet bare, I went to find Lisa to get my tour of the property and see what other information I could weasel out of her.

And try to get together a plan to escape.

CHAPTER 8
LUCA

I hit the button that would lower the shades over the window behind my desk. The sun was beginning to set, and it was glaring off my monitor. Not that I was getting anything done.

I couldn't stop thinking about Veda. More than once, I wanted to get up and go check on her. See how she was doing. Make sure she'd eaten and check the bruises my hands had left on her neck. I rubbed my jaw, wondering if I should call in my private physician to look at her. Then I expelled a harsh breath, pushing down any lingering feelings of guilt, or at least I tried.

Suddenly, I threw my arm across my desk in a rush of anger, knocking my keyboard and papers to the floor. I didn't know who I was angry with, Veda or myself. With a curse, I sat back in my chair and scrubbed my face with my hands. I couldn't get attached to this woman.

I could NOT.

And what the fuck was it about her that made her haunt me the way she did after knowing her all of a day?

Rising from my chair, I walked over to the side table in the corner of my office. On it was a bottle of my favorite whiskey and four glasses. I filled one glass to the top and swallowed it down before refilling it and taking it with me back to my desk.

Thirty minutes ago, I discovered the real Nicole had gone on a "vacation" to Mexico, which had not been a vacation at all, but a stint at an in-patient rehab across the border where no one would know who she was. I found this strange, as Veda had never mentioned her sister having a drug problem during our conversation. But I would ask her as soon as I had more information.

Twenty-five minutes ago, I'd put in a phone call to my only friend in the cartel to see what he could find out. And now I was waiting to hear back.

Right on cue, my cell phone rang. I finished off my drink and set my empty glass on the table before I walked back to my desk and picked up my phone. "Yeah."

"*Hola, mi amigo,*" a gruff voice said on the other end of the line.

"What did you find out?"

"I found your girl," he told me.

"So, she's still in Mexico."

"If you can say that."

"I don't have time for this fucking shit, Rene. Is she there or not?"

"She is," he said. "Or at least her body is. She was found in an alley near Puerto Vallarta. As of this moment, the body has not been identified. From the condition she was in, it might take them a while."

There was a sudden sharp pain in the center of my forehead. Closing my eyes, I tried to rub it away. "Are you fucking kidding me?"

"I'm not, *mi amigo*. Unfortunately."

My head fell back on my shoulders and I lowered the phone, staring at the ceiling like the answer to how to get myself out of this mess would magically appear in the paint. "Fuck me."

"Do you need me to take care of this for you?" Rene's voice came to me from a distance in the quiet room.

I thought for a moment, then put the phone back to my ear. "Make the body disappear, and I'll make it worth your while when I'm reinstated as your contact here."

"Done." Rene didn't even pause to think about it. "I know you're good for it or my sister wouldn't have loved you as she did."

"Rene," I said with a gruff warning in my voice.

"I know, I know, you don't like to talk about her." There was a pause. "I also know that you would go back and do it all over again if you could."

"I totally would," I said softly. So softly I didn't know that he'd heard me. Just then, something caught my eye on my computer monitor, pulling me from my memories. The camera feed to the main part of the house. I watched as Veda walked across the room, and wondered where she was going. "And don't worry about this. I have a backup plan."

There was silence on the other end of the line. And then only, "You get the son of a bitch for me. I want you to make him suffer. And then I want him dead, Luca. You hear me? I've waited long enough."

"I will," I promised. The line went dead. I laid my cellphone back on the desk, then blew out a lungful of air, long and slow this time. Moments in time flashed through my head like lightning in a storm.

Maria, all dark eyes and dark hair and soft Spanish accent, smiling at me over breakfast. Another vision of her with a shotgun in her hands, standing beside her brother. Maria laughing. Maria singing. Maria dancing around my kitchen in nothing but her bra and panties, trying to drag me into it...

I'd fallen for her fast and hard. And in the process, I'd become soft.

Another memory flashed through my mind. This one of Maria straddling me, her naked body slick with sweat, full breasts bouncing, and her head thrown back in pleasure as she rode me on the couch inside the warehouse. Again, I heard a *pop* and saw her head fly forward, her eyes wide with surprise for a single heartbeat before they became dull and sightless as the blood trickled down her face from the single hole between them. I knew the moment her life force faded away. Felt it leave her, no matter how hard I tried to hang on.

A knock on the door pulled me from the nightmare that continued to plague me every day and night. I blinked hard, bringing my focus back to my life now. "Come in," I called.

Tristan walked into my office, his cell phone to his ear. I eyed his dark suit as I waited patiently for him to finish talking. I was one of the few people who knew how many scars it hid. Most from knives and bullets. But there were some he wouldn't talk about. Not even to me or Enzo.

"It's done," he said when he got off the phone. "No one will find that body when the cartel gets done with it."

"Perfect." I sat forward, indicating for him to sit in the chair across from me. "So, now..." I hesitated, but only for a moment, "now we convince Veda to become her sister."

"Will you be able to do that?"

I caught the double meaning behind the question. "I have no choice," I told him. "Not if I want my position back in this family. Not if I want the respect of my father." *Not if I want to stay alive.* The words went unspoken between us. Mario getting away with what he'd done had gone on long enough, and only because some members of the family were torn as to how to handle his betrayal. My father most of all. It wasn't every day a boss had to decide on one son over another.

"Are you going to tell her about her sister?"

I leaned one elbow on the arm of my chair as I thought about that. "It wouldn't be right to keep it from her, and knowing the truth might help convince her to do things my way. Especially if she thinks it will help her stay alive."

"It's a shame," Tristan told me.

I narrowed my eyes, knowing where he was going before he said it. "I can't afford to have feelings about this."

"I know," he told me. "I'm just saying it's a shame. Veda has a lot of spark. She's a good match for you."

There was a lot more than "spark" to her. She was strong, and she was a fighter, yes. But there was something else. Something I wanted to explore more, if only we had the time. I sensed that she would not only be a worthy opponent, as Tristan had just said, but a worthy partner. She had fire.

And I wanted to make her burn.

I rose from my chair and pulled my jacket on. "Keep on the happenings with the cartel. Let me know when they've finished the job and there's not so much as a toenail left of Nicole to be found."

"I'm on it," Tristan said, rising with me. Then he followed me from the room as I went to go find Veda, heading off in the opposite direction. It took me a while, but I finally found her standing at the railing of the balcony off of the main floor.

She glanced over her shoulder when I opened the sliding door. But upon seeing it was me, she turned back to the burning colors of the sunset and proceeded to ignore me. I joined her at the railing, not one to back down from a challenge.

"How is your throat?" I asked her.

"What the fuck do you care?"

Taking her arm, I spun her away from the railing to face me and gently lifted her chin with my other hand. Bruises mottled the sides of her neck where my fingers had pressed into her skin. My gut twisted at this reminder of the violence that overtook me more often than I'd like to admit. Without thinking about what I was doing, I pressed a kiss to the darkest area.

Veda sucked in a breath, her body going completely still before she quickly backed away. I released her. Reluctantly.

"I have news," I told her. My tone brought her eyes back around to me. She searched my face as she waited to hear what I had to say.

"It's about your sister."

"You found her." It wasn't a question.

"I did."

I couldn't quite read the expression on her face. There was more I needed to say, of course, but I was having a hard time getting the words to come out.

"That was quick," she finally said. "But I guess I shouldn't be surprised."

"We found her in Mexico." I paused, not wanting to be the cause of the grief I knew she was about to experience, no matter how much she liked to give off the impression that she didn't care. How could she not? Nicole was her twin. And family was all that was there for you in the end. As she started to turn back to the railing, I said, "Your sister is dead, Veda."

She didn't respond at first. She didn't move. She just stared out at the sunset. "What did you say?" she finally asked without looking at me.

I told her again, adding that she had supposedly checked into a rehab there.

She made a sound, something between a laugh and a sob and a gasp of disbelief. "That's not possible." She shook her head. "My sister didn't do drugs."

"I'm so sorry," I told her, and I was surprised to find that I actually meant it. "I don't know the whole story yet, but I'll find out."

Veda stared at me, searching my eyes for lies. And when she found nothing, her face crumpled as tears swiftly filled her eyes. Violently, she shook her head. "No. NO. I don't fucking believe you!"

I didn't bother to argue with her. She had seen the truth in my expression. She knew it was true.

Finally, she stopped trying to deny it. Backing away a step, then two, she slapped a hand over her mouth to try to stifle the scream that tore from her throat as her legs gave out and she collapsed.

I caught her before she hit the balcony, gathering her up in my arms and carrying her to one of the chairs. Sitting her on my lap, I held her tight, but even I couldn't contain the explosion of grief that burst from her. Her sobs wracked through me, her entire body convulsing violently with each one, a slave to her heartbreak. I rubbed her back and let her cry. She didn't even notice when Lisa opened the patio door, concern etched on her face. I waved her away, certain Veda wouldn't want anyone else to see her like this. She popped back out with a box of tissues, then disappeared inside the house.

Veda cried until the front of my shirt was soaked with her tears and she was too exhausted to continue. Even so, I expected her to jump out of my lap as soon as she realized who was holding her, but she didn't. She stayed where she was, her blonde head tucked under my chin, and accepted the tissue I offered. "How did it happen?" she whispered.

"I don't know. There was very little information available to me. Only that she was found outside of Puerto Vallarta." This was the truth, although I had my own thoughts about it. "I've taken care of her." I left out the part that "taken care of her" meant I'd ordered the cartel to grind her up into tiny fragments and soak her in acid.

Now I just had to keep Veda away from the phones so she didn't try to call anyone. Did they have other close family members? I didn't even know. I hadn't gotten that far yet. My main goal had been to grab Nicole, and when Enzo had called me and told me they had a window of opportunity when they'd seen her go up to the apartment alone, I'd told him to jump on it, that we would take care of the rest later.

Softly this time, Veda began to cry again.

"Is there anyone you need to call?" I asked. Not that I would allow her to contact anyone, but I needed to know.

Veda sniffed. "I..." She had to pause as the tears came again. "Our parents. My best friend."

"What about other family members? Friends?"

She shook her head. "Nobody who would really care."

That was all I could get out of her before I lost her to her grief again.

We sat there for a long time as I held her, her body wracked with sobs until her voice was hoarse and she passed out, exhausted, with her head against my shoulder. Every once in a while, a shuddering sob would roll through her.

Steadying her against me, I got up from the chair. Lisa saw me coming from where she was dusting the shelves and ran over to open the door.

"Go on home," I told her quietly. "And tell Enzo the same. Tristan can remain at his position by the front door."

"What about dinner, Mr. Morelli? You need to eat something."

I smiled at her as I shifted Veda to a more comfortable position in my arms. "I'll make a sandwich. And I don't know that Veda will want anything tonight."

"Ok." She didn't sound convinced, but she didn't pry. "Well, there's some soup in the fridge I made earlier to save myself some time tonight. You can heat that up for the both of you."

I was already walking away. "Thank you. Have a good night, Lisa."

"Yes, sir. Call me if you need anything."

I left her to do as I'd asked, confident my orders would be carried out exactly as I'd said. Finding Lisa had been one of the best things I'd ever done. She was a bit odd at times, or maybe quirky was a better word, but I trusted her *and* her husband implicitly. And not just because they knew I wouldn't pause to put a bullet through them at the first sign of disloyalty. They were too grateful for what I did for them, and Lisa was the type of person who was as loyal as they come, as long as you treated her right.

So, I made sure to treat her and her husband very well. And over the years, she'd gotten to know me and how I liked to run things. Now I barely knew she was around most of the time unless I needed her.

I reached my room and laid Veda down on the bed. Then I grabbed an extra blanket from the closet and spread it out over her.

"Luca?"

Her whisper came through the darkness, so softly I wasn't sure it wasn't just a figment of my imagination. I paused halfway to the door, cocking my ear toward the bed.

"Would you stay?"

I didn't respond right away. There were things I needed to do. First and foremost being to figure out how the hell I was going to get Veda to agree to pretend to be her dead sister without fighting me every goddamned step of the way. Walking back to the bed, I looked down at her in the dim light from the hall. She was curled up in a ball with her knees drawn up in a fetal position. Her face was shiny with tears, and the pillow was gripped in her fists so tight her knuckles were white. Something moved in my chest, seeing her in so much pain. Something that was better left cold and hard. "I can call Lisa back to sit with you."

"I don't want Lisa," she said in a small voice. "I don't want to have to tell her..." The words caught on a sob.

"I can tell her for you."

She closed her eyes as the tears came again, but I didn't miss the flash of disbelief and rejection right before she did.

That thing in my chest moved again.

With a great sigh, I told her, "Give me a moment." I went into the bathroom and closed the door, took a piss, and washed my hands. As I passed the mirror, I caught my reflection and gave myself a glare of warning.

I could not fall for this woman. I could not afford to feel anything for her at all. Veda was a means to an end. That was all.

However, if holding her together while she was being ripped apart by her sister's death somehow beheld her to me, then I would do it.

Closing the door to the bedroom, I kicked off my shoes and got onto the bed, still in my dress pants and button down. There was no need to tempt myself more than I already had last night. I don't know what had come over me when I'd insisted she sleep in my room with me. As a matter of fact, I had told Lisa earlier to prepare the spare room down the hall from mine. Enzo and Tristan could take turns guarding the door, and either one of them—or Lisa—could keep an eye on her at all times when she wasn't in her room. Although I hated to put more work on them, it was going to be necessary. For my own sanity.

As soon as she felt the mattress dip, Veda rolled toward me and snuggled up against my side. I let her do it, hoping she would fall asleep and I could sneak out.

Her hand slipped under my shirt, and I hissed in a breath when she touched the bare skin of my stomach. I grabbed her wrist, stopping her from going any farther. "What are you doing?"

"Please, Luca." She sounded so sad. So lost.

Knowing I shouldn't. Knowing what it would cost me if I allowed this to happen, I closed my eyes...

And released her arm.

CHAPTER 9

VEDA

The first wave of grief had left me completely numb. As dead as my sister. Although my heart still beat and I could feel the scratch of Luca's collar against my cheek, inside, there was nothing. I was an empty void.

But before I fell into this blessed numbness, there was pain. Pain that tore through me with razor-sharp claws, ripping me open and leaving raw, bleeding wounds before condensing in my center, where it screamed for release until I couldn't hold it in any longer.

Oh my god, Nicole is gone!

I wished I could believe it wasn't true. I tried to tell myself that he was lying to me. There was no proof. That he was only telling me this so he could make me a token in his sick game, moving me around the board at will.

But he wasn't lying. I knew that was true like I knew my own name, although I couldn't tell you how. And now half of me was gone, a gaping hole in the middle of my chest. How the hell was I supposed to tell my parents? And what the fuck was I supposed to say? I didn't even know what happened to her.

And in not knowing, my imagination went wild. Images of my twin—who looked so much like me—lying dead in an alley somewhere in Mexico, a needle hanging out of her arm and trash strewn around her, and her purse dumped out everywhere. Or worse, raped and murdered, her naked body twisted and bloody and thrown into a landfill or buried in the woods.

The pain clenched my insides again, squeezing my heart until I couldn't take it anymore and everything shut down, leaving me where I was now. Comfortably numb. I would ask him to tell me as soon as he knew more. But not now. I couldn't bear to hear it now.

Luca laid down beside me, and I instinctively turned toward him. Unlike me, he was warm. He was alive.

And I suddenly wanted to be alive, too.

I wanted to feel something besides the pain.

So, I didn't think about what I was doing. I don't think I was capable of processing anything, even if I wanted to.

I was dead inside. Like my sister.

But I wanted to be alive. And he was so warm.

"What are doing?"

"Please, Luca." *Please don't fight me. Don't deny me this. I just want to forget, if only for a short time.*

After a moment's hesitation, he let go of my wrist.

My heart began to pound as I ran my palm over the hard muscles of his abs and chest, feeling the texture of the soft, curly hair in the center. Luca was a good deal older than me, and he had the body of a fully matured man, not someone who was barely more than a boy. I pressed my hand over his heart. A sign of life where I had none. With a moan, I curled myself around his hard body, soaking in his heat. I was so cold. I wanted to crawl beneath his skin, sink into him until I didn't exist anymore except as a part of him.

His hand gripped the back of my neck and brought my face to his. "Nothing will change if you fuck me, Veda."

"I know." And I didn't care.

I only had time to suck in a quick breath before his lips crashed down on mine, taking what I wanted to give him with brute force and bruising my mouth in the process. In the space of an instant, I was no longer in control. Luca was. He possessed me like he possessed everything and everyone else here, growling deep in his throat as he demanded entrance with his tongue.

I opened for him without a second thought. *Yes. Yes. This is what I want.*

The world and all of its horrors disappeared, and there was nothing but Luca. His scent filled my nose, like clean laundry and dark spice, and he tasted like whiskey as he ravaged my mouth. Rolling to his side, he wrapped himself around me, shutting out the reason I was here.

Shutting out the pain. With lips and teeth and tongue, he drove everything else from my mind.

And still, I needed more.

With a shove against his shoulder, I pushed him onto his back and crawled over his body so I could straddle him. He was thick and hard between my legs, even with our clothes between us. Instinctively, I pressed myself against his chest and rocked my hips so I could feel more of him against me.

Without breaking off our kiss, he suddenly sat up, taking me with him, and flipped me over onto my back. He kissed me once, twice, and then he was gone.

"Luca?" I couldn't help the panic in my voice as I reached out and met nothing but air.

"Shhh...I'm here."

I heard the rustle of clothing. "I can't see you." There was a note of panic in my voice I couldn't contain.

A moment later, the lamp beside the bed came on.

Luca's shirt was gone, but I only caught a glimpse of the broad shoulders and muscular form I'd already seen but hadn't fully appreciated before his lips were on mine again, his hard body pressing me down into the bed, holding in the pain that threatened to burst through the numbness at any moment. I ran my hands over his back, feeling the muscle shift beneath my palms as he held himself over me. Then he was moving, nipping at my bottom lip, my jaw, working his way over to my ear where he whispered, "I've wanted to touch you like this since the moment I first saw you."

I could only whimper in response as he trailed gentle kisses down my throat, pausing when he came to the bruises he'd left. There, he lingered, and although I knew he would never say it, I got the impression he didn't like seeing the evidence of what he'd done.

Pulling the shirt I was wearing aside, he moved down over my collarbone and tried to go lower. Then, with a sound of impatience, he rose over me and pulled my shirt up and off with quick, impatient jerks.

I wasn't wearing a bra. I only had the one I was wearing when he'd brought me here, and I had no idea what he'd done with the clothes I'd had on that night. As he sat back on his heels and looked at me as though he was seeing me for the first time, I held my breath, my body trembling, my focus completely on him.

Luca's tongue wet his bottom lip as he stared at me, then he cupped one of my breasts, his palm rough with calluses. He squeezed, hefting the weight in his hand before pinching the nipple and releasing it to do the same on the other side. Bending over me, he sucked my nipple into his mouth, hot and wet and demanding as he teased the nub until it was painfully hard and I was squirming on the bed beneath him.

Streaks of pleasure shot through my body, filling the emptiness, replacing the pain. My blood roared in my ears, telling me I was alive, that I was still here. And right now, I wanted to be here. I wanted to feel everything Luca demanded of me.

His teeth were sharp as he played with my breasts, biting the tender skin, and then laving the wound with his warm, wet tongue until they were overly sensitized and straining toward him for more. Only then did he begin to kiss his way down over my stomach. Lower and lower, until the waistband of my shorts stopped him.

I lifted my hips, my pulse racing and my breath coming in gasps, begging him with my body to keep going. I wanted to feel his mouth on me more than I wanted my next breath.

Luca untied my shorts, sliding them down over my hips and ass and dropping them off the side of the bed. Then he stood to take off his pants, his blue eyes never leaving me.

As the raw need of his stare hit me, I drew in on myself, feeling suddenly vulnerable. But I couldn't keep my eyes from him as he slowly unzipped his pants and pushed them down over his narrow hips and lean, powerful thighs and stepped out of them, leaving him wearing only black boxer briefs. My eyes dropped down to the bulge there. He was long and thick and hard, the wide head of his cock poking out of the waistband of his briefs.

"Open your legs for me, Veda."

My heart sped up in my chest, and I glanced toward the lamp he'd turned on. But it was on the other side of the bed. I was too exposed. A rabbit laid out for a lion.

"Veda." There was a warning in his voice.

But as much as I wanted this, I couldn't do it. I don't know why. I've never been shy about my body or sex, but being with Luca was different. I didn't want to just give in to him. Not about this. I needed this to be on my terms. He left me with so little control when it came to anything about my life since he'd brought me here, but this, giving him my body, was something I could have control over.

But I was so wrong.

CHAPTER 10
LUCA

I was going to come just looking at her.

God help me.

Over my boxer briefs, I squeezed my fist around my cock to the point of pain in a vain attempt to get myself under control. And I thought I'd succeeded...until she got that gleam in her eyes. The one that told me she was about to be difficult.

A drop of cum appeared at the tip, running down to wet my fingers.

Veda's eyes locked on to my hand, now wrapped around the swollen head, and her tongue wet her lips.

My blood rushed beneath my skin, and I grew impossibly hard. This woman was going to unman me with nothing but a look. "Let me tell you how this is going to go, Veda. I'm going to tell you what I want, and you're going to do it, or I'll take you over my knee and spank your ass until you learn how to do as you're told. Do you understand me? Now open your fucking legs."

Her mouth fell open and her beautiful chest rose and fell with quick pants. She had a beauty mark near the nipple of her left breast, and a light spray of freckles just under her collarbone. Her stomach wasn't quite flat but soft, curving slightly just above her pussy. Her hips were full and round. Just the way I liked my women. Dark blonde curls hid her secrets from me, but after tonight there would be no more hiding. "This is the last time I'm telling you. Open. Your. Legs."

She shook her head and started to sit up.

A slow smile spread across my face. I actually would've been surprised if she'd obeyed me. Surprised and disappointed.

With her eyes still on my cock, she scooted to the edge of the bed and reached for me, but I grabbed both of her hands before she could and sat down beside her, dragging her with me until she was lying across my lap. Ass up.

When she realized what was happening, she started to struggle, trying to get up, but I held her down with an arm behind her head and threw one of my legs over hers, trapping her and leaving my right hand free. I adjusted her a bit so her round ass was in perfect striking range.

"Luca, don't you dare!" Her voice was laced with panic.

"You should've opened your legs when I told you to." My palm landed on her ass with a sharp slap. To her credit, she didn't yell or scream, only stiffened with a sharp intake of breath. I immediately rubbed my palm over the area, soothing the sting as I watched the blood rise to the surface of her soft skin. Fuck, she had a perfect ass.

I lifted my hand and slapped her other cheek, then did the same again. I continued my punishment until her entire ass was an angry shade of pink and she was panting and cursing me. "You have a beautiful ass, Veda." I skimmed my palm over one cheek, then the other, feeling the heat rise from her skin. Then I dipped two fingers between her legs, sliding them into the silky heat between her folds. She was soaking wet.

Veda moaned aloud when I pushed one finger inside of her, then spread the silky moisture up to her clit and back, rimming her ass. She writhed on my lap, trying to both push back against my hand and get away, and I growled a warning low in my throat, my cock pulsing against her stomach with every hard beat of my heart.

I *wanted* this woman. No, I didn't just want to fuck her. I wanted to own her. *Needed* to own her. I wanted to lock her in my room where no one could take her from me, just so I could do this whenever I wanted to. I wanted to fuck her until she didn't have the energy to challenge me, then let her sleep until she woke up full of fire again.

Lifting my leg, I released hers. "Spread your legs for me, Veda." My voice was raspy, my breath coming fast and hard, as she slid her foot across the floor and opened for me.

Yes. This is what I wanted. What I needed. What *she* needed. If only to remember what it felt like to live.

I slapped her pussy and then her ass again. And again. Until she was squirming against me, teasing my cock with every strike. Then, and only then, did I give her what she wanted, sliding two fingers inside of her and pumping them in and out fast and hard a few times before finding her clit again. She made no sound when I touched her there, massaging the hard nub as I spread my palm over her until my thumb was at the entrance of her ass, her face shoved into the mattress.

Slowly, I pushed it inside of her. "I want to hear you come," I ordered. "Come for me, *vita.*" *My life.* Veda shook her head violently even as her body convulsed as she came, so hard I had to press down with my other arm to keep her on my lap.

She was still shuddering when I slid my arms under her and moved her onto her stomach on the bed with her legs dangling over the side. Kneeling behind her, I spread her ass with my hands and put my mouth on her pussy, tasting her pleasure and urging her on.

"Luca..."

My name was both a curse and a prayer, and the best thing I'd ever heard come out of her mouth. I fucked her with my tongue, spreading her thighs wider so I could get to her clit, then replacing my tongue with my fingers, first in her cunt and then in her ass as she fought the things I made her feel. I had an overwhelming urge to be inside of her everywhere I could, until I was a part of her and she of me.

I knew she was only acting out of grief. She needed something to hang onto in this world, something to make her forget, even temporarily, and I was the only thing that happened to be available. I knew how ravaged she was on the inside. How it tore you up until you felt nothing at all. Until you were desperate to feel something besides the pain. I'd been willing to do anything to make it stop. Booze. Drugs. Sex. Fights. It made no difference to me. As long as I could feel something else for a while besides that soul-shattering loss.

Veda was using me right now. But the thing was, I didn't fucking care...

My heart pounded in my ears as a heavy weight settled in my chest.

Or, fuck. Maybe I did.

Goddammit.

Pressing my forehead against her sweet ass, I closed my eyes and let her scent fill my nose.

After a few seconds, she spoke. "Luca? What's wrong? Why are you stopping?"

I just shook my head. I didn't have an answer for her, because I had no fucking idea where this raw need had come from.

"Please don't stop," she whispered, her voice thick with tears. "Luca. Please. *Please.*" The last came out as nothing more than a high-pitched plea. "Pl...pl...pl...ease..."

As sobs once again wracked her body, I pulled on my pants, leaving them unbuttoned as I gathered the rest of my clothes and walked out of the room.

CHAPTER 11

VEDA

R age roared through my body until I trembled with it. It heated my face as I stomped down the hall away from Luca's room, trying doorknobs as I went, wearing only the comforter off the bed because I refused...fucking *refused*...to put on anything of his.

Technically, the comforter was his, too. I knew that. But since it only touched the sheets and not his bare skin, it didn't count. Or, at least, that's how I rationalized it to myself in my broken mind.

He'd left me. Just fucking left me there. But first he'd made me come harder than I ever had in my life. Then the bastard had pulled on his pants, grabbed his shirt off the floor, and strolled out of the room like nothing at all had fucking happened.

Left me on the bed with my bare ass in the air, my skin hot and throbbing from his hand, my overly sensitive breasts aching, and my pussy clenched with the need to be fucked until I had a concussion from my head smashing into the headboard.

But it wasn't just the physical craving. Or the embarrassment of him walking out while I was lying naked on his bed. After everything he'd taken from me, I'd asked for one thing. Just this one fucking thing. I'd needed him to help me forget. If only for a little while. Just for the night.

And he'd fucking left.

I found an empty bedroom at last and slammed the door behind me. Then I locked the doorknob, just for good measure. Flicking on the light, I looked around.

The walls were a light peach. The floors the same marble as throughout the rest of the house, only partially covered by a darker peach area rug. There was a single, queen-sized bed with a cream-colored quilted headboard and matching comforter, a weathered oak nightstand and a matching dresser. A window took up most of the wall to my right, and there was another door to my left. Hopefully to a bathroom, because I never planned to come out again.

Turning the light back off, I threw myself on the bed, not really caring if this was someone else's room. Although I didn't see how it could be. No one else lived here that I was aware of. Slowly, the anger at Luca faded away as the pain of my sister's death flooded back in and the tears began to flow.

It was much, much later when I reached for the lamp, looking around for a phone. I needed to call my parents. But there was no line of communication out of this fucking room. Of course.

I'm not sure how long I'd been sitting there staring vacantly at the floor when there was a knock at the door. "Ms. Calbert? It's Lisa." When I didn't answer, she knocked again. "Veda?" And then, quieter, "Please let me in before Mr. Morelli finds me here."

Getting up, I unlocked the door and let her in.

The moment she was inside and the door was shut again, she grabbed me in a hug, comforter and all. "I'm so sorry about your sister," she told me softly. "Tristan told me what happened."

I'd thought I was all cried out. Thought there were no more tears left. But I was wrong. The loss of my twin rose up inside of me like a volcano, overflowing with hot, wet tears beneath the kindness of her condolences.

"I hated her, you know," I said when I could talk again.

She frowned, shaking her head. "You didn't. Why would you say something like that?"

"Because she was a bitch."

"And you're not?"

I heard the humor in her voice and pulled back, sniffing and wiping my face. Honestly, from what she'd seen of me so far, it wasn't an unreasonable question. "No. Not like her. If I'm a bitch, it's because someone has pushed me to that point. Nicole is—was—a bitch by nature. Even to me." You would think out of everyone in the world her twin sister would've been spared from her nasty attitude, but if anything, she'd treated me worse than everyone else.

I often wondered what I'd done to her to make her hate me so much.

Maybe hate wasn't the right word. She tolerated me, but I always had the feeling she resented my existence in her world. And yet she would never let me leave.

"How about a drink?" Lisa asked. "Something strong. And then I'll sit with you as long as you'd like." She smiled, brushing my hair from my face. "You shouldn't be alone right now."

"I need to call my parents," I told her. "Do you have a phone I could use?"

I could tell immediately from the look on her face the answer was no. However, all she said was, "Let me get those drinks and I'll see what I can do."

I nodded. After all, what more could I hope for in this fucked up place? "You wouldn't happen to have some clothes I could borrow, would you?" I asked. "I don't know what happened to the ones I had on when I got here, and I can't wear his." Lisa was slightly taller than me, and maybe ten or fifteen pounds lighter, but surely she had something that stretched.

She searched my face, curious for secrets I wasn't ready to tell. "That I *can* do," she said. "Hang tight. I'll be right back."

After she left, I went back over to the bed and sat down, tears tracking silently down my cheeks as I tried to fight back the horrors of the day. Memories of Nicole and me growing up flashed through my head like an old movie reel. Right up until she turned fifteen and decided she had better things to do than hang out with her "stupid" sister who couldn't keep up with her. Not in school. Not in life.

That's where the movie always stopped. I didn't miss the person Nicole had become after that. It was a horrible thing to say, but it was the truth.

Lisa knocked on the door again before letting herself in. She had alcohol, two glasses, and some kind of clothing thrown over her arm, but no phone.

When I raised my red, burning eyes to hers, she just shook her head. "I'm sorry, I asked Mr. Morelli, but we can't take the chance the call will be traced back here."

We, she'd said. She was one of *them*. It was a good thing for me to remember. "I thought you didn't want him to know you were here."

She had the decency to look ashamed. "I kind of told you a bit of a lie about that. He asked me to come check on you."

I waited to see how I would feel about that, but there was nothing.

"But I have these." She held out the pants and T-shirt she had over her arm, both black. "It's just an extra set of mine I keep here in case I slosh gravy all over myself or something. We can order you some clothes when you feel up to it."

"I want *my* clothes back," I told her as I held onto the comforter with one hand and took the clothes with the other. "The perfectly good clothes I was wearing when I got here. But thank you," I added with a nod at the clothes.

But she just gave me a small smile. "We'll get you some new stuff. Of course, Mr. Morelli will have to approve the purchases." She wouldn't look at me as she said it.

I stared at her for a long moment, wondering if this was her trying to be nice or if she was just carrying out his orders in a subtle way, but I didn't have the energy to fight right now, so I just turned away and went into the bathroom to put on the clothes she'd brought me, and I was grateful. The pants went past my ankles and were a little tight in my ass, and the T-shirt was a little tight across my chest, but they fit well enough. Luckily, the material was super soft, so the chafing was minimal on both my red ass and my still sensitive nipples. There was no bra or underwear, but at least I was covered.

When I came back out, Lisa handed me a glass with some type of amber-colored alcohol. Whiskey, if I had to guess.

But honestly, it could've been horse piss and I wouldn't have cared. Not if it made me drunk enough to forget the last twenty-four hours. "Thank you," I whispered.

"You're welcome," she answered with a small smile that dripped with sympathy.

Maybe I *was* a bitch, because that smile made me want to slap her. Avoiding her eyes, I brought the glass to my lips, welcoming the burn it left behind as I swallowed half of it in one gulp. To Lisa's credit, she didn't tell me to slow down, just let me do what I needed to do.

Filling up my glass again, she sat beside me on the bed, cradling her own between her two hands after taking a small sip. I studied her from the corner of my eye. "Isn't *Mr. Morelli*"—I tried to keep the disgust out of my voice but didn't know how successful I was—"going to be pissed you're drinking on the job?"

"Technically, I'm off," she told me. "So, there's really nothing he can say." She paused. "Well, maybe a little bit of something about the fact that I took his favorite whiskey from his office." She waved one hand in the air, as though to chase away any negative vibes she'd brought on herself. "But I'm sure he must have more hidden away somewhere."

"So, you've got some balls on you," I said.

She let out a small laugh. "I guess."

I watched her again as she sipped on her drink. "Aren't you afraid of him?"

She seemed surprised by my question. "Mr. Morelli?" When I nodded, she shook her head. "No, I'm not. Not at all."

"He's going to kill me, you know," I told her in a flat voice, beyond caring at this point.

To her credit, she didn't look away, but held my gaze as she said, "I really don't think he will."

"You do know he's in the mafia, right? And the kind of things they do?"

Lisa nodded. "I do. And Mr. Morelli will do what he has to, when he has to. But only that."

This took me aback, and for a moment I just stared at her. "Which is why he's going to kill me," I insisted. I didn't know why I was pushing the subject with her. Maybe I just wanted her to see him, really see him, for the kind of man he was. Or perhaps I needed her to either confirm my fears were justified or give me a damn good solid reason why they weren't. Telling me, "He's not that kind of man..." just didn't cut it. "You don't believe me," I said when she just sat there looking down at her drink.

She sighed. "I think that right now he believes he will have to do that eventually, yes. For his own safety." She turned to me, placing one hand on the bed close to my leg. "But, Veda. I honestly believe that when it comes down to it, he won't do it. He won't kill an innocent woman."

"What other option does he have, Lisa?" I finished my second glass and looked around for the bottle, feeling a bit dazed. I realized I was exhausted, now that the alcohol was doing its job and the numbness was coming back. "And since we're being all truthful and shit, I'm kind of okay with that right now."

"You don't mean that," she said with more emotion in her voice than I'd ever heard from her. "Things will get better, Veda. Eventually. It's just going to take some time."

I took a drink and handed her the bottle. Maybe. Maybe not. I'd never lived life without my sister in it. Sometimes I liked her, most of the time I'd hated her, but she was always there. Always. I never thought I'd have to go through it without her. "Do you have more whiskey?" I asked her. "Actually, could you just leave me a bottle?" In other words, I was done being sociable. I was being rude, but I didn't care.

"No, hon. I'm not going to do that."

I swallowed as the tears welled up again. "I'm just so tired," I told her by way of explanation.

"I know you are."

"I just want to sleep."

"I know."

She didn't get me that bottle, but she sat with me until I passed out, glass still in my hand and tears streaming silently down my cheeks.

At some point during the night, I woke up. It was still dark outside. Or maybe I'd slept through the day and into the next. There was a tray on the nightstand with a bowl of something, some crusty bread, and a glass of water.

My mouth tasted like something had crawled in there and died, and I had to pee. So, I got up and took care of business and then rinsed my mouth out with some mouthwash I found under the sink. Ignoring the tray, I locked the bedroom door again and crawled into bed, turning my back to the food.

Closing my eyes, I tried to go back to sleep. And when I couldn't, I opened them again. My sister was lying in bed beside me. Her face, so familiar to me, not five inches from my own. I didn't question if it was real or not. I didn't really care.

I gave her a teary smile.

She didn't smile back.

CHAPTER 12
LUCA

Two weeks had passed since we'd almost fucked. And Veda hadn't once come out of the room she'd taken over without my permission.

At Enzo's suggestion, with Tristan backing him up, I'd left her alone and allowed her to grieve, but the waiting was driving me mad. I wasn't a patient man, though I was trying to be. I'd allowed her to move out of my room. I'd given her time to deal with the worst of her grief. But now I needed her to get her shit together.

My brother had come home to Austin.

I found Lisa in the kitchen just as she was starting to make dinner. "Why don't you go on home," I told her.

"Are you sure? I don't mind making something for you real quick."

"No, really. It's okay. I'll take care of dinner."

"What about Veda? Ms. Calbert?" she corrected.

"I'll handle Veda tonight."

Lisa stilled, looking down at the floor. I watched her, more curious than anything at this reaction from her, but she only raised her chin and said, "She's only been eating what she needs to stay alive. And barely that. I keep making her different things, hoping something will catch her interest enough to get a decent meal down her, but so far I haven't had much luck."

"I'll get her to eat," I promised. "Do you have the key to her room?"

Another moment's hesitation, and then she reached into her pocket and handed it over. "I only use it to leave food and drinks on the nightstand for her."

There was a warning in her tone. I chose to ignore it. "Thank you," I said.

She looked like she was about to say more, but she correctly thought better of it, for she only gave me a tight smile and went to gather her things. "Have a good night, Mr. Morelli. And good luck."

I saw her out and then went to my room to change into a pair of jeans and a T-shirt before I went back to the kitchen. Lisa had a package of chicken breasts thawing in the refrigerator, so I took it out to make my famous chicken piccata. Turning on some soothing music, I opened a bottle of wine and got to work.

It took me a little over an hour, and in that entire time I hadn't heard a peep from the direction of Veda's room. I'd been in and out of the house a lot these last couple of weeks while she'd kept herself locked away, dealing with some things I've been ignoring since I'd brought her here. I always left either Enzo or Tristan here with her, the only two I trusted to keep her safe, just in case she decided to come out.

When the food was ready, I left it warming in the oven and went to get her. As I expected, the door was locked when I arrived at her room. I knocked softly. "Veda? Are you awake? You need to eat something." When there was no response, I knocked a little harder. "Veda. Open the goddamn door."

I knew she was grieving. I knew she was hurting. But life went on, and I wasn't going to let her fucking starve herself to death. I knocked again. "Veda! I'm coming in." Pulling the key from the front pocket of my jeans, I unlocked the door and let myself in.

The room was all shadows with the setting sun, and it took me a moment to find her curled up beneath the heavy comforter, small as a child. "Veda?" Shoving the key back into my pocket, I walked over to the bed. Through the cracks in the blinds, I could see her blonde hair covering the top half of her face, and the comforter covered the rest.

I found the lamp on the nightstand and turned it on, keeping it dim. "Hey," I said softly, reaching out to touch her arm, though I'd told myself I wouldn't. "We need to get you out of this bed. I made dinner for us, and it would be an insult to my mother if you at least didn't come try it." She didn't move or respond in any way.

Carefully, almost afraid of what I would find, I took the comforter away from her face and brushed her hair back out of the way. It was limp, weighed down from not being washed. I laid the back of my hand against her cheek. She was warm and alive. *"Amore."* I touched her face again. "Come on now, let's get up and have something to eat."

Finally, she responded to my voice. Just a disgruntled moan, but it was better than nothing. She tried to pull the blanket back over her face. "I'm not hungry." The words were so quiet I barely heard her. Her voice raspy from disuse.

"Veda, you have to get up. You need to shower. And you need some food. I know you're hurting right now, *amore*, but it will get better. But only if you get out of this bed and continue to live." She didn't move a muscle, and I sighed. "Your sister is gone, Veda, but you're not. You're still here. You still have a life to live."

Her eyes fluttered open, and the extent of the lifelessness inside of them stopped my heart. "I don't want to live without her," she told me. "I haven't even told my parents... They don't even know..." Her words were drowned out by a fresh set of tears.

"Yes, you do. You may not feel like it right now, but you do. You still have so many things to do, Veda. Places to see. People to meet." Grimly, I steeled myself against the lies I was forced to tell her. She wouldn't experience any of those things. Not for long. But I needed her to be up and functioning.

She made a disgusted sound and closed her eyes again.

"Oh no, you don't. You can't just give up on me. I need you."

"You only need me for your sick game."

Her venomous words, filled with a sudden burst of energy, struck me right in the face. I pulled back as they ricochet around inside of me, creating fissures in my cold exterior.

She was wrong. She was so, so wrong. And as the truth of that statement hit me in the gut, it made me angry. Not at her, but at myself.

Closing my eyes momentarily, I took a breath. I was being ridiculous. I barely knew the woman. The only thing I needed was for her to get out of this disgusting bed so I could burn it.

Gritting my teeth, I yanked the blankets off of her. "Come on, Veda. You're getting up. You're getting a fucking shower. And you're eating the fucking food that's drying out in the oven while I waste my time dealing with you. Food I made with my own fucking hands." She tried to pull the blankets back up over herself, but I wouldn't allow it. "I'll shower you myself if you don't get out of this goddamn bed." Still, she didn't move.

Okay. Fine.

Sliding my arms beneath her, I lifted her and carried her toward the bathroom. She was light as a child in my arms. And that pissed me off even more. "What the fuck are you doing to yourself?" She'd lost enough weight that I could hold her in one arm as I turned on the shower. But it wasn't until I sat her under the spray fully clothed that she woke from her stupor.

Throwing her hands up in front of her face to block the spray of water, she coughed and sputtered. "What the fuck, Luca?"

"You stink," I told her. "And I'm not eating my dinner with you like this."

"Nobody asked you to," she said with a little more life in her voice. Yet she just sat there under the spray, not even trying to get up. Like she didn't have the energy to fight me with anything other than her words.

Taking off my T-shirt and jeans, I folded them neatly and got into the shower. When I laid my hands on her, I was relieved to see some of the fire return to her eyes. She fought me as I stripped her down, but she was weak from lying in bed and not eating. And when I saw her ribs and hipbones poking out of her skin, I growled low in my throat, barely containing my outburst of temper, furious at her for not taking care of herself. Grabbing the shampoo, I lathered up her long hair, rinsed it, and washed it a second time. Then I did the same with her body, scrubbing every inch, then forcing her under the spray of water to rinse.

Veda cursed me the entire time, her thin arms trying to push me away. But by the time I turned off the water, she was clean, and I was soaked. Grabbing a towel from the heated rack, I rubbed her briskly until her blood flowed and her skin was a healthy pink, and then bundled her up in it before I wrapped a second one around my waist. "Come on," I told her, grabbing my clothes.

She tried to crawl back into bed, but I headed her off and marched her down the hall to my room, where I held onto her wrist as I found her some clean, dry clothes.

"I don't want to wear your stuff!" she spit at me.

"Would you rather sit at my table naked?" I asked her calmly. "Because I don't mind. You're way too thin, but at least you still have your tits."

Her lip curled, and she pulled back her arm.

I caught it before her palm could make contact with my face. "Do NOT hit me again."

Her nostrils flared as she glared up at me. We stood, locked in a standoff, until she yanked her arm from my grasp and grabbed the clothes I held out for her. Stomping into the bathroom, she slammed the door. I heard the lock click.

I allowed her the moment of rebellion as I got myself dressed. When she came out, modestly covered in one of my shirts and some lounge pants that hung from her thin hips despite the drawstring, I walked over to her and took one of her hands in mine, forcing her to unclench her fist. Holding her hand between my two palms to warm it, I took a moment to rein in my temper. Fighting with her would not get me what I wanted—her compliance. "As I was saying, I made us dinner. And I would appreciate it if you kept me company. I thought we could talk." It was a command, not an invitation, but she seemed to take it as one anyway.

Her deadened eyes traveled over my face. Once. Twice. Before she finally said, "Fine."

Releasing her hand, I indicated for her to lead the way down to the dining room. I followed her closely, ready to catch her if her strength gave out.

"Sit, Veda. Please," I added when we arrived at the table. After a pause, she took a seat. I got the food from the oven and dished it out onto two plates, then I poured her some wine and sat down across from her. "I have a new offer for you," I told her.

"The only thing I want from you is for you to let me go."

"You know I can't do that."

"You *can*," she emphasized. "You just won't."

"Fair enough," I told her. "I will *not* let you go. But perhaps we can come to an agreement that will work for both of us."

"Like, what kind of agreement?" she asked after a pause.

"Eat something, and I'll tell you."

With a heavy sigh and a great show of reluctance, she picked up her fork and knife and cut off a small piece of chicken and put it in her mouth, chewing it slowly, then swallowing as though she were trying to choke down a tennis ball. I chose to ignore her rude manners, and just be happy she was eating something. I took a bite of my own chicken just to make sure it hadn't dried out too much in the oven, but no, it was fine. Better than fine, as a matter of fact. Closing my eyes, I savored the taste. I hadn't made my mother's chicken piccata in a long time. God rest her soul.

"You said you would tell me if I ate something. I ate something."

I glanced up at her over the short expanse of the table. She was sitting with her hands in her lap, her food untouched in front of her except for the one small bite I'd forced her to take. "I'll tell you what, for every bite you take, I'll tell you something new, or let you ask a question, if you prefer. But if your plate isn't clean when we are done, this new deal I'm about to offer you is off the table."

"I'm really just not hungry, Luca."

There was no fight in her tone this time, but at least there was still a little light in her eyes. "This isn't up for negotiation," I told her.

She stared at me for a long moment, then picked up her fork and stabbed it into the broccoli with quite a bit more viciousness than was necessary, even if one wasn't a fan of that particular vegetable. Without taking her eyes from me, she shoved it into her mouth and begin to chew.

"So," I began. "I've been thinking about things while you've been holed up in the spare room." Taking another bite of chicken, I made her wait as I chewed and swallowed. "I understand that it's not fair for me to make demands of you without offering you something in return. Therefore, I'm giving you this chance, this *one* chance, to strike a deal with me. So, tell me, Veda, what is something that you would like out of our arrangement?"

"I want to know how you plan to use me. And I want to live," she said immediately.

Although I had expected that answer, it still struck me dumb for a second when she said it. Letting her live...for now, yes. I needed her to live. *For now.* The first demand was harder to answer without giving away my answer to the second. "I want you to be your sister."

She didn't seem surprised by my response. "What exactly will that entail?" Lifting her fork and knife, she cut off another piece of chicken and put it in her mouth.

"I will need you to transform into Nicole. New clothes. New hair. Perhaps contacts, as I think her eyes are bluer than yours. Am I right?"

She nodded. "They are. She's always been more..." she looked around for the word she was looking for, "vibrant than me."

"I seriously doubt that," I told her.

She harrumphed as she looked down at her plate and moved the broccoli around with her fork. "You didn't know my sister."

"I didn't need to. I saw her interview on TV. It was enough to see she didn't hold a candle to you."

Her fork slowed, but that was the only reaction she gave to my honest words.

Seeing she was uncomfortable, I continued our original discussion. "Once everything is done, you'll no longer be Veda, except when we're alone in this house. As Nicole, you'll accompany me when I need you to, wherever I need you to, and you'll have nothing but fucking love for me when others are around."

"And then?"

Then you will die in front of the man I have grown to hate. I understood her relationship with her sister more than she knew. "I'm still working the rest of it out."

She didn't believe me. I hadn't expected her to. My Veda was much more intelligent than that. She caught my gaze, her trembling lower lip giving her away, despite the steel in her gray eyes. "I want to live, Luca."

But that was a very dangerous option for me, which meant it wasn't an option at all...unless...maybe...there was something I could hold over her. "Your parents," I said. "Where do they live?" I threw it out there casually, taking a bite of my veggies.

Her fork dropped to her plate with a clang. "I'm not telling you that."

Ignoring her outburst, I briefly closed my eyes, savoring the taste of the food. The broccoli was steamed to perfection. "You have to give me something, Veda, for me to even consider this. If you were in my shoes, knowing what you know, and our places were reversed, would you just let me go willy-nilly out into the world again?"

I had to give her credit, for she thought about it. Really thought about it. She even managed to hold her composure as she said, "No. I wouldn't."

"Then you understand the position you're putting me in?"

She gave me a nod, her hands clenching into fists where they were resting on the table.

"Eat," I told her. After a few tense seconds, she did as I demanded, and I continued our conversation. "Let's set that one aside for now, to be discussed again at a later time. What else would you like?"

"My own clothes."

Ah, this one was easy. "Done. But you're only to wear them when you're here. From what I've seen of your sister, you two appear to have different tastes in clothes. When you go out with me, you'll wear what she would."

"We do," she admitted quietly. "She liked to think of herself as quite the fashionista."

"And what is your style, Veda?"

"Hot Texas Summer."

My lips twitched in amusement. "What else would you like?"

"I want to call my parents."

I started to shake my head, but she quickly jumped in.

"I won't tell them anything about you," she swore. "But I normally call them at least every other week or so. They'll worry about me." Silently, she pleaded with her eyes. "I just want to let them know I'm okay. And I need to tell them about Nicole..." Her words tapered off and her eyes filled with tears.

"You can't call them. And you can't tell them about your sister. Not yet," I added. Because I understood. I truly did.

Her eyes shot to mine. "They deserve to know. You asked me who I needed to call..."

"I only asked you that so you would tell me who might be looking for you. Of course, you can't call them." I sat forward in my chair. "What sense would that make, Veda? If you told anyone your sister is dead, how would I play my game?"

"You fucking bastard." Her voice was cold and quiet.

I smiled and set my fork down, then I leaned back in my chair and met her look with one of my own.

"Do we have an agreement, then? You convince everyone you're Nicole, and I will buy you some clothes and leave your parents be. For now. The rest will be discussed at a later date. Yes?"

She stared at me across the table, her jaw set and her eyes cold. As a single tear rolled down her cheek, she nodded.

CHAPTER 13

VEDA

L ater that night as I headed back to my room, unescorted for once, I watched him as I climbed the stairs to the second floor.

He stood in the main room, talking to the other guy, the one who wore sunglasses all the time. As if he felt my attention on him, Luca suddenly stopped speaking, his head snapping up and his eyes locking on mine. His head tilted slightly to the side, and he slid his hands into the front pockets of his jeans. The other guy took up the conversation, but he may as well have been talking to the wall.

I found myself a prisoner of that intense stare. My breath caught in my chest, and I stumbled, catching myself just in time with a hand on the railing. Heat crept up my neck and into my face, and I shot him a dirty look. I caught a smile teasing the corners of his mouth before I looked away.

"Veda."

I stopped where I was at the sound of my name, one hand hanging onto the railing and my eyes on the step in front of me.

"Tomorrow, I'll take you shopping to get you a few things until we can bring in a personal shopper."

Taken by surprise, I looked down at him, feeling small despite my greater height. "Why can't Lisa take me?"

"Lisa has other things to do."

I waited for him to say more, but he didn't. Just pulled his hands out of his pockets and crossed his arms over his chest as he went back to his discussion with Sunglasses.

Dismissed, I tried not to stare at the way his arms bulged with muscle beneath the short sleeves of his T-shirt. Or the way my body reacted to the sight of him, all mature confidence with a healthy serving of pure arrogance.

I made it to my room without any further mishaps, locking the door behind me. But once inside, I took one look at the grimy bed I'd been living in for the past two weeks and marched into the bathroom to get my toothbrush. He'd said he had, like, five spare rooms or something ridiculous, right? Surely, there was another one available for me to use.

On the other side of the second floor, I found two more rooms, one with a balcony and one without. I chose the balcony room, even though the decor wasn't as girly, mostly blues and browns. Brushing my teeth, I crawled into the clean bed, feeling only the slightest bit of guilt at leaving the other room so disgusting. I didn't think I'd be able to sleep, but to my surprise, I soon felt myself drifting off, my belly comfortably full for the first time in weeks.

I don't know what time it was when I was jolted from a dream. No, not a dream, a nightmare. My sister, her legs broken at strange angles and her jaw hanging crooked, chased me down a rural road. She was calling my name. Begging me to help her. But I was too scared. That thing...it wasn't my sister. And no matter how fast I ran, she was always there, right behind me. Sucking in a breath, I prepared to scream as I felt arms slide around me.

"Shhhh...it's just me."

I was lifted from the bed and cradled against a hard chest. In my semi-conscious state, I smelled laundry soap and dark spice. I immediately stopped struggling, my eyes flying to his face as I struggled to slow my breathing, barely lit by the soft light coming in through the open door. He didn't look happy he'd found me.

"Jesus fucking Christ, Veda. I thought you were gone."

Where the hell would I go? According to him, I'd get shot, or worse—bitten by a snake, the moment I stepped foot outside the door. "Put me down."

He wouldn't look at me, but I could tell he was pissed from the way his jaw was clenched so hard the muscles jumped in his cheeks as he took me from the room.

"Where are you taking me?" No response. "Dammit, Luca. Put me down!" Tired of his manhandling me, I started to struggle again, landing a good backfist to his mouth before he tossed me up in his arms and threw me over his shoulder, holding down my legs so I couldn't kick him.

My hands, however, were free.

Balling them up into fists, I let loose on him, landing punches everywhere I could. "Put. Me. DOWN!" Why the hell didn't I lock my bedroom door?

He didn't so much as flinch as he strode down the hall with me pounding on his back. Less than a minute later, he threw me onto his bed. I landed on my back, bouncing once, and I was back on my feet. But I didn't make it two feet before he stopped me with a hand gripping my jaw, forcing me to look at him.

"I thought you were *gone*," he repeated through his clenched teeth.

I stared up at him, mutinous, my hands around his wrist as I tried, and failed, to pull his hand from my face.

"I thought someone found out about you. I thought they came in here and fucking *took* you, Veda." Anger darkened his blue eyes to a stormy gray.

"You're hurting me," I gritted out.

He stared at me hard, his chest rising and falling as though he'd just beaten the hell out of that punching bag downstairs. But after a moment, he released me and backed up a step, resting his hands on his narrow hips as he took a deep breath. He didn't offer me an apology for all the manhandling, but I really didn't expect one.

Without a word, I turned and walked away.

"Where the fuck are you going?"

I didn't stop. "Back to my room."

He was in front of me before I could make it to the door he'd kicked closed when he'd brought me in here. "No."

"No?" Was this guy fucking kidding me? "No," I repeated. Then I just shook my head. "Get out of my way, Luca."

"No. You're staying here. With me."

"Why?" *You didn't want me. You* left *me.*

He drew back, like that was the last question he'd expected to hear. Then his eyes narrowed on me. "Because I said so."

"Now you sound like my mother. Or my father. Depending on how horrendous my crime was at the time."

"I don't care who I sound like. I'm done letting you mope. You're staying in here from now on."

I crossed my arms over my chest, tilting my head as I studied him, trying to gauge his mood. His eyes dropped to my braless chest, my breasts pushed up from my arms, before rising back to my face. I left them there. Let him fucking look. "Give me a good reason why," I pushed him.

"There are plenty of spare rooms in this giant house. And absolutely no reason at all I should stay in this one. With you."

"Other than the fact that I said this is where you'll be sleeping. With me," he emphasized.

Oh, my god. There was no reasoning with this guy. Again, I tried to walk around him. Only this time, when he stuck out an arm to stop me, I batted it away and kept going. My hand was on the door handle when he spun me around and pressed me back against the door, holding me there with his body.

I could feel the hard length of him against my stomach as he gently kissed my face where his hand had gripped me. My pulse picked up as my blood rushed through my veins, the muscles low in my stomach clenching. As though he could sense my reaction to him, he pressed his lips against the artery in my throat. And at that moment, I wouldn't have been surprised in the least if I suddenly felt fangs sink deep into my flesh.

"Stay with me," he commanded.

Chills ran down my spine as his deep voice vibrated against my throat. My legs went weak, and moisture pooled between my thighs. I was weak. God, I was so weak. I couldn't control the way my body reacted to him. But I could control what I did about it. Shaking my head, I said, "No," proud that my voice came out strong and steady.

He stilled, then pulled back until he could look at me. "I'm not asking, Veda."

His big body surrounded me, a hand on either side of my head, caging me in. I felt his heart beat fast and hard beneath my palms where they lay flat against his warm chest. A flair of panic shot through me. "So, it's rape, then? I thought you didn't do that?"

"I wouldn't have to," he told me, and I wanted to slap the cocky smirk from his face, even though he was right. It wouldn't take much to convince me to let him fuck me. However, after what had happened last time...yeah, no. He'd rejected me in more ways than one that night. There was no way in hell I would give him the chance to do it again, no matter how much I wanted it. This was a game I wouldn't win, and I knew it.

This man had taken my life from me, but I refused to give him my body.

We stayed deadlocked for a long time, or perhaps it just felt like an eternity as my traitorous body warred with my mind. *It's nothing but a bad case of Stockholm syndrome*, I told myself. I should feel nothing but pure loathing for this man. Yet, here I was, lusting after him like a mare in heat, even though I knew that giving myself to him would break me to a point I wouldn't be able to put myself back together again.

Finally, he pushed off the door and took a step back, his blue eyes like burning steel as they locked onto my face.

Quickly, before he changed his mind, I turned and yanked open the door.

As I hurried down the hall, I heard him on the phone. "Enzo, I need you to stand guard outside of the blue bedroom with the balcony. Veda is sleeping in there." A pause. "No, she can go wherever she wants, just...keep an eye on her. Thank you."

I heard his door shut none too quietly, and then I was around the corner and heading down the opposite hall to my new room. Somehow, I managed to hold in the sobs until I was alone in the big, empty room.

CHAPTER 14
LUCA

I woke up the following morning with a hard-on from hell. Gritting my teeth, I stepped into the shower, releasing a moan when the warm spray hit my overly sensitive cock. This woman made me feel like a fucking eighteen-year-old kid who couldn't control himself around a pretty girl.

With a muttered curse, I grabbed the shampoo and dumped some on my head, working it through my short hair, scrubbing my scalp so hard it was a wonder there was any hair left when I was finished. Closing my eyes, I stuck my head under the spray to rinse.

Big fucking mistake.

All I saw behind my closed lids were Veda's bare breasts, soapy water dripping from the tips of her extended nipples. Her full, rounded ass across my lap, the smooth skin pink from my palm. Veda staring up at me with fire and ice in her eyes, defying me. Challenging me. Pushing me away.

Even though I'd only kept her in my bed that first night, I'd missed her these past weeks. It didn't make any fucking sense, but there it was. The smell of my shampoo reminded me of my face buried in her thick, wavy, blonde hair as she slept, tucked perfectly into my body like she was made to be there. Every time I worked out, our fight flashed through my mind. Followed by my own guilt for what I'd done. This...obsession...was shit I'd never felt before. Not even with Maria. Of course, Maria had never spit foul words at me. And she'd never raised a hand to me. Not that she hadn't wanted to, but she'd known better than to push me.

Veda didn't give a fucking damn.

Thinking about the way her eyes snapped at me in anger sent a fresh wave of blood rushing to my cock. I went to grab the soap and sucked air in through my teeth as the spray of water hit me again. *"Fuuuck..."*

My hand went to my sex, and I gripped the engorged length in my fist, sliding to the head and squeezing. Chills shot up my spine as I slid back down to the base, tightening my grip as I tried to gain some type of control. Closing my eyes again, I imagined Veda on her knees in front of me, her gorgeous lips wrapped around my swollen cock, doing what my hand was doing, and had to lock my knees to keep from falling to the shower floor.

Giving up the fight, I braced one arm against the wall and dropped my head, my hips thrusting my cock in and out of my fist, imagining it was Veda's mouth. My balls began to feel heavy, the base of my cock tensing, preparing, as I fucked my own hand. And then it was there...

Turning my head, I bit into the muscle of my shoulder to muffle my shout as I came, my orgasm shooting through me fast and hard, my cock pulsing as cum ran down my hand and got washed away in the hot water.

I stayed how I was for a long time, breathing heavy through my mouth and waiting for my heartbeat to slow. When I felt like I could move again, I grabbed the soap and methodically finished washing and shaving, my mind empty of everything but the woman who was causing so much distraction in my life. I couldn't even take a shower without jacking off since the day I'd brought her here.

Shutting off the water, I grabbed my towel, drying myself with short, rough strokes.

I was going to kill her when this was all over. In front of Mario. I was going to make her hurt, with words and blood, and then I was going to shoot her in the head right in front of him. And I could not let the needs of my fucking dick get in the way of that. It was what my brother deserved. It was the way our family worked. An eye for an eye. Then it would be up to our father to decide what to do with him after that.

But dammit. I didn't want to.

Wrapping the towel around my waist, I went over to the sink and brushed my teeth, trying to get my head on straight. I couldn't afford to be soft about this. That's what had gotten me where I was to begin with. Veda was not for me. She was a pawn in my game. Nothing more. I spit into the sink and rinsed my toothbrush, then stared at myself in the mirror.

That didn't mean I couldn't fuck her while I had her.

For a second, I cursed Nicole. If she hadn't been so fucking stupid, it would be her here and not her sister. Then maybe, someday, I would've found Veda in a different place. A different time. And she never would've seen this side of the man I am.

I scrubbed my face with my hands, then gave my head a shake before finger combing my hair back from my forehead, narrowing my eyes at the ever-encroaching gray strands that seemed to multiply by the day. Walking into my room, I glanced at the bed, rumpled from my restless night.

And empty.

Today was Thursday. I needed to have Veda under control by Saturday. There was a birthday party, and we were going. Well, Nicole and I were going. People were going to be there. People who would make sure word got back to Mario that his fiancée was now with me. I smiled at the thought. I couldn't wait to see the shock on his face when he saw the woman he thought was dead was alive and well and thoroughly fucked by me.

I had no doubt my brother was behind Nicole's "overdose." And as Veda had never met him, I hoped he didn't know about her either. The sisters didn't seem to talk about each other much. There wasn't a photo to be found of Nicole with Veda beside her. At least none that Tristan had found. Only a few of her following behind the actress with her head down and her face turned away from the cameras. According to the press, Veda was no one, no better than a servant, and therefore not worth the effort to find out who she was.

All of this would work in my favor when the time came to confront Mario.

Pulling a random pair of black slacks and a white button-down out of my closet, I got dressed, opting for my more comfortable dress shoes, since I'd be taking Veda shopping today. But first, I had a few calls to make and other things to take care of.

Enzo was waiting for me in my office.

"Veda?" I asked as soon as I saw him. Not because I was concerned. I just wanted to gauge her mood.

"She's in the gym," he told me. "Tristan is keeping an eye on her."

I stopped behind my desk, looking at him in surprise before I sat down. "Well, at least she's out of her room."

"Maybe she's gettin' in shape to kick your ass."

I grunted in response. Enzo was one of the few people allowed to talk to me so casually. And only because we'd been together since school. He knew me well. Probably too well. But he always had my back. And I, his. I trusted him with my life. Hitting the intercom on my desk, I called the kitchen, where I'd seen Lisa bustling around on my way to my office. "Lisa, make sure Veda is showered and dressed and ready to go shopping in three hours, please."

"Yes, sir, Mr. Morelli," her pleasant voice responded right away. "Should I bring in your breakfast?"

"Yes. Thank you. For Enzo, too."

"Of course."

Logging onto my computer, I checked the business accounts for the strip clubs we owned downtown, making sure the expected deposits had been made. I'd check in with the managers later today and make sure everything was running smooth. We laundered our drug money through them, so it was important they didn't reflect that. Lisa came and went, dropping off our food and coffee. I was halfway through my egg white omelet before I realized Enzo wasn't talking. Nor was he eating.

I set down my fork, looking at him around my monitor. "What is it?"

He took his sunglasses off the top of his head and set them on the desk. "I have concerns, Luca."

His way of telling me he didn't approve of something I was doing. "About?"

"Veda."

Leaning back in my chair, I laced my fingers over my stomach. "What about her?"

"I don't like this."

I sighed and took another bite of my breakfast. I'd known this was coming. Eventually. Deep down inside, Enzo had a soft heart, and an unusual set of morals. Unusual for someone in his position, that is. "We've discussed this," I told him.

"No, Luca. We discussed doing this to Mario's actual wife-to-be. Not her sister. A woman who has absolutely nothing to do with him. She's never even met him."

"I find that hard to believe." This was exactly what I'd just been thinking to myself, and yet I found myself arguing with him anyway.

"Why?"

I set down my fork and stared across the expanse of my desk at my longtime friend. "Veda is Nicole's sister. Her *twin* sister."

"But she is *not* Nicole."

"She's been mourning her sister's death for weeks. I find that an unusual way for someone to act if they weren't close."

"Maybe it's not her sister's death she's mourning, but her own."

I closed my mouth, whatever I'd been about to say dying on my tongue, and threw myself back in my chair. This, too, had come to me in the dark hours of the night. And yet to hear it said out loud..."Fuck."

Convinced he'd finally gotten through to me, Enzo relaxed and took a bite of the breakfast Lisa had brought for him. "So, what are we going to do with her?" he asked around a mouthful of food. "We can't just let her go."

"Of course I'm not letting her go. The plan hasn't changed." His eyes flew to my face, his gaze sharp as glass. I explained, "Veda is a small sacrifice for the overall greater good, Enz. You know this has to happen. *Our* lives depend on me getting a leg up in this organization again. And to do that, I have to cripple Mario. And Veda is the path to that end."

He shook his head, stubborn as always. "There's gotta be another way."

"There's not."

"You could just kill him."

"Not good enough." Not after what he'd done to me. To Maria. "Besides, that's my father's final call. Not mine. And he hasn't given me the go ahead."

Tension rode in the air between us. That wasn't unusual. Whereas Tristan was prone to just do what I told him—not because he was easily swayed, but because he honestly didn't give a fuck about anyone or anything except the two of us in this room—Enzo and I often didn't see eye to eye. It's what kept me from getting too cocky, and I appreciated him telling me his side of things. But I wouldn't be swayed. Not on this. I needed to see Mario suffer as I had. And it was nothing less than he deserved.

"Goddammit, Luca."

"Finish your breakfast," I told him in a kinder voice. "And then go get some sleep. I'm just going to run over these numbers, and then I'm taking Veda shopping."

"Why not send her with Lisa? Tristan can go with them."

"Because I don't trust her not to make a break for it, and because I'm taking this as an opportunity to be seen before the party." I paused. "And to win her over to my side of things."

"What if she won't play along?"

I was glad to see he'd given up on the subject of letting her go. At least for now. "She will."

Exactly three hours later on the dot, I was standing in the middle of the great room, waiting for Veda. I heard her bedroom door close, and a few seconds later she was walking swiftly down the walkway to the stairs. When she saw me waiting for her, she stopped.

I watched her debate what to do, until finally her desire to get out of this house won out over whatever apprehension she had about spending time with me, and she gracefully descended the stairs. My eyes roamed over her. She was dressed in a similar black outfit as the day I took her out of her self-imposed prison. Lisa must've loaned them to her. The material stretched across her tits and ass, but luckily it was thick enough that it wasn't see-through.

"I don't want you to take me shopping," she informed me when she reached the bottom, her sneakered feet silent on the marble floors.

"It's not your decision to make," I informed her. "You want clothes to wear? Then you're going to let me take you shopping. If not, you can keep running around in the same borrowed clothes. It's your choice."

She narrowed her eyes and crossed her arms over her chest, leaning her weight to one side and cocking out her hip. "Now, why would you take time out of your busy day to do something so mundane as take me shopping?" she mused.

"I've told you. I don't trust you. Are you ready?"

After a pause, she sighed and walked toward the front door, and I followed.

"Why can't I wear my other clothes? You know, the ones I had on when I got here." Her tone was deceptively calm, but I knew better.

"Your clothes are here, but you won't be wearing them."

"Why the hell not?"

I came up behind her and pressed my hand against the door as she tried to open it, not missing the way she stiffened when she felt me behind her. "Rule number one.

While we're out in public, you will speak to me with respect. Rule number two. You will know what you need to know; no more, no less."

"I don't understand why I can't just wear my own fucking clothes," she gritted out. "Instead of walking around in hand-me-downs like a homeless person."

I decided to give her this one. "Because *if*, by some miracle on your part, you were actually able to escape, I don't want you being seen in the same clothes you may have been reported missing in. If there *is* anyone who actually misses you. Do you understand now?"

Her chest rose and fell with each shallow breath. "Yes."

"Good. Now let's go find you some new things to wear."

CHAPTER 15

VEDA

The ride into the city was unusually silent. I sat in the backseat of a blacked-out SUV, as far from Luca as I could get. One of the guys that took me from my sister's condo drove, his eyes constantly scanning the area around us and his gun lying on the seat beside him. It was the first thing I'd noticed when Luca had opened the door for me and I'd climbed into the vehicle.

"Go ahead and try," he'd told me when I froze halfway into the car. "I dare you."

Gauging the time it would take me to reach over the armrest and grab it and my odds of reaching it before either of them stopped me, I sat down in my seat and pulled the seatbelt across my lap. I could try it, but I wouldn't succeed, so why waste the energy. I refused to look at him as he shut the door and climbed in beside me. Lacing my fingers together in my lap, I turned to look out the window.

And that was how I'd remained the entire ride.

It gave me some time to think, though, now that I'd been forcibly pulled from my cocoon of self-pity and grief. Watching the scenery roll by as we made our way from the hill country to the city proper of Austin, the reality of what my life was now settled like a weight in my chest, and I came to accept the fact that there was no way I was getting away from this man beside me. He was going to use me for his game of revenge, and when he was finished, when I had no use to him anymore, he was going to kill me. I had no doubt about it.

Unless…

Unless there was a way to change his mind.

From the short time I'd been there in his house, there were a few things I'd noticed. The most important being that Luca had very few people in his inner circle. But the people he considered his, he treated well, and if what Lisa told me was true, he would do anything for them. So, my new plan was simple. So simple, I didn't know why I hadn't thought of it until now.

Instead of fighting to get away from him, I would fight my way into his inner circle. And hopefully once I got in there, he would want to keep me. It wasn't the life I'd planned, or one that I wanted, but it could be worse. And it was better than not being alive at all.

But I had to do it carefully. Luca wasn't stupid. If I suddenly changed my attitude toward him, he would definitely suspect something was off. My change of heart had to seem natural. So, as hard as it would be, I needed to push down my fear and anger and get to know him. Let him get to know me.

Let him fall in love with me.

It sounded arrogant, even to myself, but it was my only chance. I already knew he was attracted to me physically. And he seemed to enjoy what my father had always lovingly called my "spirited" personality, as long as I didn't push it too far. Or maybe because I did. Maybe there weren't many people who had the balls to get in his face, and that was why he liked it. Perhaps he needed a bit of a challenge in his life.

But I had to do this carefully. So very, very carefully.

We pulled over near some bougie stores on 2nd Street. I hopped out of the SUV before Luca could come around to help me, and nearly got run over by a bicycle in my haste.

I'd barely jumped out of the way before Luca had a hand wrapped around my arm and was pulling me onto the sidewalk. "Wait for me next time," he growled.

"I'm perfectly capable of getting out of a car by myself," I spit right back at him. "I'm not a child."

"Then stop acting like one. You could've been seriously hurt."

"Well," I drawled. "We can't have that, now can we? Because that would totally fuck up everything. For *you*."

We stared each other down until people started to walk slower, throwing curious looks our way as they passed us. When he noticed, Luca gave me a tight smile, offering me his arm like the gentlemen I knew he was anything but. "Shall we?"

Reluctantly, I laid my hand in the bend of his elbow, bracing myself for the tingle that always rippled through me whenever I touched him.

"What would you like to look at first?" he asked me as we strolled along the sidewalk.

I almost told him I didn't care, but then I remembered my plan, and I took a deep breath. He was making an effort to be decent. The least I could do was to do the same. "It irks me that you have to buy me clothes," I admitted honestly.

He looked at me, a shock of surprise in his blue eyes. "Don't do that, *amore*. I can more than afford to buy you a few things, so you'll be more comfortable. I would've done it weeks ago if you hadn't locked yourself in that room."

"I'd be more comfortable if I was in my own home with my own things."

The weight of his stare was heavy on my face, and then he faced forward again. "I understand that," he said quietly, to my surprise, "but it's not going to happen."

I waited for him to say more. To say he was sorry. Or that he'd changed his mind. Stupid, hopeful things.

He didn't.

"How about in here?" he asked.

Looking at the window display, I saw a few items that looked like they were right up my alley. "I'll make you a deal," I told him, turning to look up at him.

He cocked his head, waiting, his eyes resting on my mouth for a moment before they rose to meet my own.

"I'll let you buy me stuff now, on the condition that I'll pay you back for it. Someday."

He started to shake his head, "That's—"

"Stop," I said, holding up my hand before he could say anything else. Like how I would never have the chance to pay him back because I was never going back to my old life. "Just give me this one. Please."

His eyes narrowed, but he surprised me again. "Okay."

"You agree?"

He gave me a nod.

I felt like I'd just taken a step toward my plan, small as it was, and I smiled. "Then let's go shopping."

His eyes traveled over every inch of my face, but I must've been pretty convincing, for the tension left his jaw. "After you," he told me.

Walking into the shop with Luca on my heels, I immediately went to the sales rack, as was my habit.

"You don't have to do that, Veda. Cost is no object."

"Shouldn't you be calling me Nicole?" I kept my eyes on the clothes in front of me, not daring to look at him as I pulled out a summer dress that was blush pink and laced down the back. Very much my sister's style. I blinked away tears as I imagined her in it.

He was quiet for so long I wondered if I'd already pushed it too far. Finally, he said, "No. Not here." And that was the extent of his explanation. "Try that on," he ordered.

I'd been about to put the dress back on the rack. Instead, I held it up and looked at it again. "This?"

He nodded.

"But I have nowhere to wear it."

"You will. Soon. There's a party I'd like to take you to."

"What party?" My stomach slightly nauseous, I laid the dress over my arm and continued to look through the racks as though it didn't bother me at all that I would be taking on the identity of my dead sister "soon."

"A birthday party for someone in my family. And I need you to go with me." I could tell he expected me to argue with him.

I glanced at him from the corner of my eye. "You mean you need Nicole to go with you." Somehow, I managed to keep my voice steady.

He stilled for a moment, then continued his perusal through the clothes rack in front of him. "Yes," he told me. "It's on Saturday. Two days from now."

I digested that piece of information. I would go with him, of course. I couldn't make him fall in love with me if I refused to spend time with him. Refused to play along in his game. But...*carefully, Veda.* "What if I don't want to go?" I pulled out a pair of pants. Checking them out, I made a face and put them back. "You can force me," I answered before he could say it, "but then wouldn't you be afraid I'd tell everyone who I really am?"

His response was immediate. "No. Not at all. We made a deal, you and I. And I trust you will live up to your end of it."

Wandering over to another rack of clothes, I glanced at him from the corner of my eye. If he was bluffing, he was very good at it.

"Come on, Veda. You're an intelligent woman. You know what would have to happen if you tried something like that. Besides," he added. "You'll be surrounded by my family. You won't have an opportunity to rat me out, and even if you did, they wouldn't believe you. Or care."

Good to know. I grabbed a few more things and headed to the dressing room. When I realized Luca was following me, I stopped and turned, frowning at him. "I'm going to the dressing room."

A smile teased the corners of his mouth. "So am I."

"Uh, no. You're not. You're not allowed in there with me."

"Sara!" Luca called to the single employee in the store.

The girl behind the counter hustled right on over, all knees and elbows in her shift dress and walking like a deer on her five-inch heels. "Yes, Mr. Morelli?"

Without taking his eyes from me, he said, "Lock the front door. I'd like us to have the store to ourselves."

"Sure thing." And off she went to do exactly as he'd said, even shooing out another customer who'd just come in.

Biting back the comment that was on the tip of my tongue, I tried for an impressed expression. "I feel so *Pretty Woman*-ish right now."

"I'd like to see what I'm buying before it walks out of this store."

I didn't miss his meaning. Turning on my heel, I found an unlocked room and hung the clothes I'd found inside.

"Try the pink dress first," he ordered, then sat down in a chair near the 3-way mirror.

Shutting the door so he couldn't see me, I flipped him off as I kicked off my shoes, then got undressed. In no hurry to obey my new master, I tried on three pairs of shorts, a few vintage-looking, short-sleeved tops in blues and greens and golds, and a pair of pants to wear around the house. They were bright green, baggy, and comfortable, and after only a short argument with Luca, they were mine. Apparently, he's not a fan of the color.

"The dress, Veda."

Making a face at his patient tone, I removed the damn thing from its hanger, slipped it over my head and tugged it down. I had no bra, but I wouldn't be able to wear one with this anyway. It was pretty, the openness of the back setting off the more modest front nicely. The skirt was an A-line that landed right at my knees. The bodice darted to flatter my figure. The only thing I couldn't reach were those darn laces.

"Let me see, Veda."

Barefoot, I opened the door and walked out.

Luca was quiet for a moment as he looked at the dress. "Turn around."

I glanced up sharply at the growl that had entered his tone.

"Turn around," he told me again, spinning his finger in a circle.

Holding the dress together where the laces gapped right above my ass, I turned around until my back was to Luca.

"Stop."

I watched in the mirror as he rose from his chair and came toward me. Brushing away my hand, he started to straighten out the laces, the backs of his knuckles skimming the bare skin of my back from the base of my spine to my neck. Everywhere he touched, I burned, little thrills of pleasure shooting straight between my legs.

"All done." His voice was low. Strained.

Dragging my eyes from his reflection, I stepped to the side to see myself fully, smoothing down the skirt and twisting to see the back before standing still again. I was a little thinner than normal, and the dress was very flattering.

"You look beautiful," he told me.

He stood so close I could feel his breath ruffle my hair. "It would help if I had shoes," I said. Luckily, the bodice was layered, and mostly hid the fact that my nipples were hard and sensitive, vying for his attention.

"Mmm." Taking a seat in the chair again, he crossed his ankle over his knee, the picture of a patient boyfriend. "We'll take that one. What else do you have?"

"Maybe one more thing." I started to walk away, but Luca stopped me with a hand on my arm. He stepped behind me, and I felt the laces loosen across my back.

"We definitely need this dress," he murmured in my ear. Sweeping my hair to the side, he lightly brushed his lips against the side of my throat, lingering there as he inhaled the scent of my skin before he released me.

A hand over my stomach to steady myself, I returned to my dressing room and nearly ripped the thing from my body, not sure what I hated more—how much Luca liked it, or the fact that what he liked wasn't me at all, but me dressed as my sister.

The only things I had left were some bras, underwear, and a swimsuit I'd grabbed without really looking at it. I'd already tried on the bras but refused to model them for him. The underwear I knew would fit. And I was loathe to try the bathing suit on after what had happened with the dress, for it also had laces. Gathering up the rest of the clothes I wanted to get, I left the suit in the dressing room and joined Luca. "Actually, this is it."

Taking the clothes from me, Luca took them to the front to pay. I stood beside him, my heart still thumping and my knees locked as he chatted pleasantly with the salesgirl.

I could still feel the brush of his lips and the rumble of his voice in my ear. It sent chills up and down my spine.

"Would you like to change?"

Snapping myself out of those obtrusive memories, I blinked up at him, and realized he was speaking to me. "What?"

"Would you like to change your clothes before we leave? Put on one of your new outfits."

I looked down to see him holding the bag out to me. "Oh! Uh, sure. Yeah, that would be great. Thanks." *What the hell are you thanking him for? Kidnapping you? Dressing you up like his doll?*

Taking the bag, I disappeared back into the dressing room and threw on my new underthings, a pair of drawstring black shorts, and a printed turquoise top. I'd have to stick with the white sneakers until I could get some different shoes.

The rest of the afternoon went by quickly, and by the time dinnertime came around, I had enough clothes to be comfortable and even a few nicer things to wear out to his blood parties, along with four new pairs of shoes.

"Are you hungry?" Luca asked me. "There's a great Italian place right down the block with some of the best pizza. We can sit outside if you like."

Actually, I was starving. And pizza was my food of choice at any time of day. "That sounds great."

The restaurant he took me to was a quaint little place with sidewalk seating, the tables shaded with umbrellas. Benches ran along the edge of the patio, and this is where Luca sat me, tucking me back into a corner and sliding in next to me. We ordered drinks and decided on a margarita pizza. I watched people walk past as we waited for our server to return with our sodas, jealous of their normal lives and wondering where they were going. Briefly...very briefly...I thought about calling out and asking for help. However, I thought I knew Luca well enough by now to know he wouldn't just let me go, and I didn't want anyone to get hurt because of me.

Taking a sip of my soda, I glanced at him out of the side of my eye as I racked my brain for something to talk about. It was hard to think with him sitting so close to me, his dark spice scent in my nose and his thigh nearly touching mine. "So, where did you grow up?"

He angled his body toward mine, one arm on the back of the bench and the other resting on the table, caging me in. Instead of answering me, his eyes narrowed. "What's this you're doing, Veda?"

Well, fuck.

CHAPTER 16
LUCA

"I'm not doing anything," she told me. "I'm just trying to make conversation."

I almost believed her.

The problem was that Veda never just "tried to make conversation." She fought with me, or didn't speak to me at all, or she was sleeping. One of the three. As a matter of fact, she'd been way too pleasant this entire afternoon. It was making my ass itch. She was trying to get on my good side. But to what purpose? This relationship, fake or not, was going to end the same way, no matter what.

However, maybe it would be fun to play *her* game for a while.

"I grew up in New York," I told her.

"You don't have an accent," she commented, waiting for me to say more. When I didn't, she asked, "And how did you get here to Texas?"

I let my fingers brush the bare skin of her upper arm, watching with something akin to fascination as goose bumps trailed in their wake. "I killed someone I shouldn't have." I watched her expression as she took that in.

She took a sip of her soda. "Oh."

"And," I continued, "there was an opportunity here for our business. So, with my father's urging, I moved to Austin."

"He was trying to get rid of you?"

I shook my head. "He was trying to keep me alive. And avoid the wrath of the Russians until he could get things under control. It was a win-win situation. Now he travels back and forth between here and New York. And when he's not here, I'm in charge."

She stirred her drink with her straw, watching the bubbles float to the surface. "I don't suppose I can ask what your business is?"

"I run strip clubs." That was the public side of my business. She didn't need to know what I did illegitimately.

Her gray eyes shot to mine. "What kind of strip clubs?"

I fought the urge to smile. "Is there more than one kind?"

"Uh, yeah. There is. There's guys. Girls. Girls who were born as guys. Guys who were born as girls..."

"Girls," I said. "I run the kind with girls. I don't care if they were born that way or not. As long as they bring in customers."

Her mouth tightened with disapproval, or maybe jealousy? "Underage girls?"

"No. That would be human trafficking. And that's a fucked up thing to do. I would never get involved in that shit. All of my girls are over eighteen, clean, and work there of their own free will."

"Glad to hear you have *some* morals, at least."

"There're a lot of things you don't know about me, *amore*." Like how every minute you're with me makes it harder and harder to remember what I have to do.

She frowned up at me. "Why do you call me that?"

"Would you rather I called you 'Nicole'?"

"Fuck no."

I lifted one eyebrow.

"Fine. Call me whatever you want."

Ah, there was that bite. I'd missed it.

The waiter came with our pizza, and she was quiet while I thanked him and put two slices on her plate.

"Did you have friends growing up?" she asked.

Flashes of blood-splattered walls ricocheted around in my head. I set down my pizza and picked up my napkin, holding it over my mouth until the feeling passed. "Yeah. I did. I had three. Now I have two." The third had had his arms and legs sawed off with a rusty chainsaw right in front of me. He hadn't lived long after that. He'd died before we could get him to a hospital.

I felt Veda's eyes on me. "I'm sorry if I brought up something I shouldn't have," she said, her voice subdued as she watched me.

Picking up my pizza, I took a bite, using the time to get my shit together. That had happened over twelve years ago, when I was still young and cocky. I wasn't either of those things anymore. "You didn't do anything," I told her.

She put her hand on my arm, the warmth of her touch dragging my head out of that blood-soaked room and back to the present. Back to her. "I'm sorry, Luca," she repeated.

I stared down at her fingers, so delicate against the muscles of my forearm. "Eat," I told her. "We need to get back to the house."

Giving my arm a squeeze, she did as I told her, not questioning me about anything else.

Jesus fucking Christ. Digging my cell out of the front pocket of my pants, I called Tristan and told him to come and get us in ten minutes. Then I flagged down the waiter and paid the bill so we could leave as soon as we were ready.

The ride back to the house was as quiet as the ride into the city. Only this time, instead of staring out the window, Veda kept glancing over at me.

Finally, I turned and looked right at her. "Stop it."

Her eyes widened and she jumped back, startled.

I took a breath. "Stop sitting there staring at me like I'm some kind of poor lost puppy. Because I'm the furthest thing from it. My life hasn't been easy, Veda. People have died. Some of them in horrific ways. But I'm still here, and I plan to remain that way. So I'll do whatever I have to do to acquire that end. Don't pity me. I'm not a man you have to pity. I've done things that would give you nightmares for months if I told you about them." I leaned toward her, picking up a strand of her hair from where it lay over her breast, brushing her nipple with the back of my fingers and smiling when it hardened. So sensitive. "And I enjoyed bathing in their blood."

Her chest rose and fell with short, sharp breaths as I ran the strands of her hair through my fingers. She was afraid. And yet her body responded to me always.

"Your hair is so soft," I murmured. "Like silk." I wanted to drape all that hair across my chest and stomach like a blanket. "Come to my room tonight."

"No," she told me immediately.

There's my feisty girl. I smiled and dropped her hair.

As we pulled up in front of the lake house, I watched her closely as I told her, "I have a few things I need to take care of tonight, so you'll have to find someone else to mouth off to."

Veda's eyes shot to me, filled with indecision. Then she said, "I can wait for you, if you'd like. Maybe we could watch a movie? Or just have a glass of wine or something? How long do you think you're going to be?"

I studied her innocent expression. Definitely up to something. "It'll be much too late. But I'll have Lisa stay and keep you company." I could see the wheels in her mind whirring a hundred miles an hour. No doubt she planned to question my employee to within an inch of her life. But I wasn't worried. Lisa was, at times, just part of the background of my home, so much so I'd forget she was there. But I didn't doubt one ounce of her loyalty. She would never betray me.

The car stopped. Getting out, I walked around to help Veda with her bags as Tristan took the car around to the garage. When we reached the upstairs, I was tempted to deposit them in my own room, and tell her she would be sleeping with me if she wanted to see them again. But in the end, I walked past my door and followed her to the guest bedroom where she'd taken up residency.

"Thank you," she told me as I set the bags on the bed. "For the clothes and dinner and everything."

"You're welcome."

I left her with her new things and headed to my office, stopping by my room to change first. Being that the only thing I really needed to do was sit in my office and sip on a whiskey while I let Veda squirm, I thought a pair of black lounge pants and a white T-shirt were perfectly suitable attire.

Barefoot, I padded down the stairs and disappeared into my office before Veda came out and saw me. Curious as to what she would do left on her own, I poured myself a drink and pulled up the camera feeds on my monitor. I could see the hall outside her room, the great room, the kitchen, the gym, and the entertainment room. Not the bedrooms or the bathrooms. Although the thought crossed my mind that I should remedy that immediately.

Ten minutes later, she left her room. She had also changed, and was now wearing one of my shirts, a pair of sleep shorts she'd gotten for herself, and some slouchy socks. I enlarged the picture on my screen and leaned forward in my chair, watching her breasts as she jogged down the stairs.

Leaning back, I palmed my growing cock as I sipped my drink. This woman did things to me just by walking.

Instead of going to find Lisa, she went directly to the front door, and I sat up in my seat, my heart pounding. I tried to think what guards were on the grounds who might see her, but I needn't have worried, she didn't open it. She only looked through the glass for a good minute, then turned away from the door. Going to the right, she walked the circumference of the room.

I settled back again as she trailed her fingers along a shelf, touching a priceless object here, examining a photo there. I was so caught up in just watching her, I almost missed it.

"Sneaky little thing, aren't you?" I murmured to myself.

As Veda wandered around the house, she would glance around every once in a while. It took me a minute to notice what she was actually doing. She was looking for cameras. And she hadn't gone to the front door just to look out. She was watching for my men.

She was testing the boundaries. Planning an escape.

I narrowed my eyes. Maybe giving her freedom to roam hadn't been the greatest idea, especially since I'd dismissed both Enzo and Tristan, wanting to be alone in the house with her.

Picking up my cell phone, I called Lisa.

"Yes, sir?"

"Have you already left?" I asked her.

"Not yet. I was just finishing a few things downstairs. Do you need me to get you something?"

"No. But would you mind hanging around for a while? I have some things to do in my office and Veda has been left to her own devices. She could use some company."

"Of course! I don't mind at all. I like Veda. Have you both eaten?"

"Yes, we ate in the city."

"I'll see if she wants some tea then."

"She's on the main floor."

"I'll find her. Have a good night, Mr. Morelli."

"You too, Lisa. And thank you."

Not two minutes later, Lisa entered the picture. I couldn't hear what she was saying, but she waved Veda toward the kitchen. Smiling, Veda followed her.

I switched screens.

Veda sat at the table while Lisa made them both some tea. They were talking, and I should've been trying to figure out what they were saying, but I couldn't take my eyes off of Veda. How relaxed she was. How openly she smiled. How she threw her head back when she laughed, and then immediately covered her mouth like she was afraid someone would hear her.

I wanted to hear her laugh like that.

They talked for a long time as I watched, until, when I was on my third whiskey, Veda couldn't hold back her yawns. Getting up from the table, she took her cup to the sink and—I assumed—told Lisa goodnight.

I followed her on the camera feed as she made her way up to the guest room and disappeared inside.

It was almost an hour later when I left my empty glass on my desk for Lisa to get in the morning and walked up the stairs. But I didn't go to my room. Instead, I kept walking to the other side of the house where Veda was sleeping.

Taking the key out of my pocket, I unlocked the door and slipped inside.

CHAPTER 17
VEDA

Something warm and wet slid across the side of my throat and I shivered, reaching for the blankets even though I wasn't cold. But someone took my wrist and pressed it down into the mattress beside my head before I could cover myself.

I rolled over onto my back as I struggled to open my eyes, to lift my other hand, but that one too was held to the bed.

"Shhh...it's only me, *amore.*"

That voice. I knew that voice. The sound of it made chills dance across my skin even as my stomach clenched with both dread and need. "Luca?"

He shifted both of my wrists to one hand, and I felt his weight settle beside me on the bed. I smelled whiskey on his breath. One of his legs was thrown over mine, pinning me down. "What are you doing?" I demanded, coming more fully awake now.

His answer was to slide his free hand under my shirt, his calloused palm rough against my stomach. "Luca—" My words were cut off as he kissed me, hard, demanding, forcing my mouth to open to him. I moaned as his tongue swept in right as he found my breast, squeezing the heavy mass of it and then pinching the nipple until my hips lifted off the mattress, seeking him out of their own accord.

Turning my head, I broke away from his mouth. "Stop," I told him as he nipped at my jaw. Ah, god. I needed him to stop, or I was going to be lost.

"You don't want me to stop," he rumbled in my ear.

"I do," I protested. This was not how my plan was supposed to go. *I* was supposed to seduce *him*. But I knew exactly what he was doing. He was calling my bluff.

Luca just chuckled softly as his hand found my other breast, the nipple straining against his palm like the little fucking traitor it was. Finding the sensitive spot between my neck and shoulder, he bit into the muscle, making me jump, then soothed it with kisses.

My breath came in pants, and moisture pooled between my legs. "Luca, please." I tried one more time.

In response, he moved his hand back down my stomach to the waistband of my shorts and easily slid beneath the loose elastic. He moaned against my neck as he pressed the heel of his hand against my womb, his fingers playing with the soft curls for a second before one finger delved between my folds. "Fuck, Veda."

I started to struggle in earnest. I didn't want him to feel how much he turned me on. This was *not* part of my plan, dammit! He was supposed to fall in love with me, not make me his willing sex slave. "Stop," I told him again, pushing against his shoulders. "Stop!"

"No," he growled, right before his lips captured mine again. Leaning over me, he used his weight to hold me still as he worked another finger between my legs. When he couldn't get as far as he wanted, he tore his mouth from mine. I felt his weight lift off of me, but before I could go anywhere, he was pulling my shorts down my legs. Then my thighs were pushed apart, and his wide shoulders were between them, his arms looping around my thighs and pulling me up to his mouth.

I cried out when I felt the first lick of his tongue. "Stop," I moaned. But he only gripped me tighter, ignoring the way I tried to push his head away. Sitting up as much as I could, I started to hit him.

His teeth sank into the inside of my thigh, catching me so much by surprise I instantly stopped. "Ow!"

"Stop fighting me." He licked me from my ass to my clit, and I froze, my breath catching. "Or I swear to god I'll tie you to this fucking bed."

The muscles low in my belly clenched tight at the thought. Then his mouth was on me again, his tongue circling my clit. My womb felt achy and full, clenching and releasing as he moaned his pleasure at the taste of me. A tear slid down my cheek as my fists gripped the comforter.

"Come for me, *amore*." His voice rumbled against my pussy.

No. No, I wouldn't. I fought it with everything I had. I wouldn't give the bastard the satisfaction, just so he could leave me again.

With a frustrated growl, he released me. But he wasn't done yet.

I heard the rasp of clothing and I scooted back on the bed, planning to jump off the other side and lock myself in the bathroom. But before I could get far, the lamp beside the bed clicked on and his hand clamped down on my ankle.

Luca pulled me back to him, flipping me over until I was on my knees with my back pressed against his front. My shirt was off and on the floor a moment later, and then he twisted us both around, sitting with his back to the headboard with me cradled between his bare legs. I felt his cock against my ass, long and thick and hard, as he wrestled down my arms and hooked his ankles over mine, spreading my legs wide. I felt seared from his heat everywhere our skin touched.

"You *will* come for me," he growled. "And then I'm going to fuck you until you won't be able to move tomorrow without remembering I own every fucking inch of you."

"No!"

One strong arm locked down over both of mine as his other hand found my pussy. My hips jumped when he touched me, my body wanting more even as I denied him.

"God, Veda, you're so fucking wet." Running his fingers through my folds, he found my clit, and I bit down on my lips to keep from crying out. "I can't wait to put my cock inside of you."

My hips were moving, encouraging him, a pain-like pleasure coming in waves low in my belly.

"Come for me, *amore*."

I shook my head.

"I want to hear you scream my name." He slapped my pussy hard, and my hips bucked up. I was pressing back against him now, trying to raise my hips to his hand. One finger pushed inside of me, his deep groan in my ear the most erotic thing I'd ever heard. "Come for me," he whispered as his fingers found me again. "I want to hear you. I want to *feel* you lose control."

I tried to stop it, I did. But I couldn't prevent the pulses of pleasure as they crashed over me. My body convulsed as he held me tight to him, but I didn't make a sound other than my harsh breathing. I refused to give him more than that.

"Fuck, Veda." His arms loosened around me, but he didn't let me go. He started to get up, to push me down onto my hands and knees, but I tried to stop him. "No! Wait."

His hand pushed me down onto my stomach. I heard the rip of foil, and then he was lifting my hips and I felt the head of his cock slide through the folds of my pussy. It caught me off guard, and I moaned.

"That's a girl." His hand squeezed my hip as he lined himself up. With one thrust he was deep inside of me, so deep I could almost taste him in my throat, and I had to shove my face into the bed to muffle my cry.

Luca stilled, and I could feel his powerful body trembling behind me. "You're so fucking tight." He let out a breath. "God, Veda."

My traitorous body pushed back against him, reveling in the sound of his groan. Wanting to hear more.

He began to move then, sliding out of me only to push back in nice and slow. His hands kneaded my hips and ass, rubbed over my back. It was no use fighting him anymore. I wanted this. Wanted him balls deep inside me. As he gained speed, I met him thrust for thrust.

Pulling out of me, he rolled me over. "I want to see you when I come inside of you," he told me. He kissed me, his hips rolling into mine. "And I want to make you come again."

I spread my legs for him, and he settled between them, nudging my entrance. My heart was racing as I looked up into his blue eyes, darkened with need. With a shove against his broad shoulders, I pushed him off of me and rolled with him until I was on top, my legs straddling his hips.

He allowed me to do it, but his eyes narrowed with suspicion. "What are you doing?"

"You can't take everything from me," I whispered, breathless. "I need to have some power here." I felt the tears come and tried to blink them away, but one slid down my cheek before I could stop it.

Luca reached up and brushed it away with his thumb, then wrapped his fist in my hair and pulled me down for a kiss. Holding me tight to his chest, he guided himself inside of me again. I rolled my hips, testing the new position.

Biting his lower lip, I forced him to let me go and pushed off his hard chest until I was sitting up. His expression was wary as I lifted up and then slid back down his length until I was seated fully. He was so deep, I felt like he was touching the end of my spine.

I started to rock my hips, faster and harder, watching Luca's face as he closed his eyes. Arching my back, I let my head fall, riding him shamelessly, my hair brushing the tops of his thighs. Beneath my palms, I felt the thunder of his heart. Heard his breaths become fast and harsh. His hands tightened on my hips.

I touched myself, gently teasing my swollen clit. Ah, god. I was going to come again.

"Luca!"

He suddenly stiffened beneath me, and I lifted my head to find him staring up at me, eyes wide. Later, I would swear I saw terror streak across his face before he rose up, wrapping me in his arms and rolling me beneath him. He was perfectly still for a long moment, deep inside of me but not moving. His hand was on the back of my head, tucking my face into his neck, his chest rising and falling on a catch with each breath.

"What's wrong? Luca?"

His big body shuddered, and then he kissed the top of my head and rolled his hips. "Hang on," he gritted out.

I couldn't move as he pounded into me, fast and deep, his hands in my hair and his weight pushing me into the bed. With one last hard thrust, he cried out as he surrendered to the needs of his body, pushing impossibly deep. And when it was over, he pulled out of me, sat back on his heels, and lifted my hips back to his mouth. With his lips and tongue and teeth, he brought me to orgasm, the pleasure crashing through me so hard I bit my tongue until I tasted blood to keep from crying out his name again.

As I fell back to the bed, exhausted, he kissed my pussy, my inner thighs, the insides of my knees, then lowered my hips and crawled up the bed, pulling me with him. Grabbing the comforter, he pulled it over us both and turned off the lamp. I heard him take off the condom and drop it in the trash beside the nightstand, then he tucked me into him, cradling my head against his chest.

"From now on, you sleep with me. I don't care which fucking bedroom we're in."

Too exhausted to argue, I relaxed against his hard body, my eyelids already closing in sleep.

CHAPTER 18
LUCA

I woke up hot. Too hot.

Opening my eyes, I found myself wrapped around Veda, our legs entangled, her body flush against mine, and her face hidden against my chest. For a long time, I lay there as she slept so trustingly against me, listening to the birds sing and watching the sky as it began to lighten with the coming sunrise.

But I didn't loosen my hold on her. If anything, I pulled her closer.

Last night I freaked out, and that surprised even me. I haven't let a woman ride my cock like that since Maria. I'd tried once, and only once, and I'd had nightmares for a week. So when Veda pushed me onto my back and climbed over me like that, my gut had clenched, but it was good. It was okay.

Until it wasn't.

The weight of her on my hips. The feel of the ends of her hair brushing my thighs. My name on her lips...

I'd lost it. For just a few seconds. I'd lost it. Looking up at her, so fucking gorgeous, her breasts bouncing and her fingers on her pussy...it was like I was back there in that warehouse. Only this time, I knew someone was there. I knew the bullet was coming. I heard the gun. But this time, *this* time, I could do something.

I didn't even think about it before I flipped her underneath me, protecting her with my body. And it took me another few seconds to remember where I was and who I was with. *Veda*. Not Maria. I wasn't in a warehouse buying drugs. I was in my home. She was safe. I was safe.

All these years later, and I was still traumatized by that shit. If anyone else found out about my reaction, I'd be laughed right into my grave. I was a Morelli. I didn't cringe. I didn't have fucking PTSD. I was stronger than that. Colder than that.

I was my father's son.

Tracing lazy circles on Veda's back, I heard her sigh in her sleep. The sound so sweet, pushing away the things I'd rather forget. Rolling over onto my back, I brought her with me, spreading her across my body like a blanket as my hands roamed over her back and ass. She had a great fucking ass. I was half tempted to ban her from wearing pants in the house just so I could watch her walk around. However, then I'd miss out on watching that ass in those tight shorts she liked.

It was a dilemma I was happy to have.

She stirred in my arms, and my cock, already hard as fuck, nudged against her hip. Sliding my hands down her thighs, I spread her legs until her knees were on either side of my hips, then maneuvered her higher on my body until I felt the heat of her on the tip of my cock. Gritting my teeth, I slid partway inside of her. I just needed to feel her with nothing between us.

And, ah, god, she felt so *fucking* good.

Her pussy clenched around me, hot and wet and tight, and I almost lost my shit right then and there. She moaned in my ear as I gripped her hips, pulling them down to meet mine, sliding in a little further. Then I waited, letting her adjust to me, my heart pounding so hard I was sure she could feel it, before I slid out and pushed back in. Nearly all the way there.

Veda was awake now. I could tell by the way her breathing hitched and how her hands fisted in the pillow on either side of my head, even though she didn't pick her head up or say a word.

Bending my knees and gripping her hips, I slammed into her, smiling when she tried to muffle her cry in the pillow. She tried to sit up, but I wrapped my arms around her, holding her to me as I fucked her so fast and hard she was nearly weeping in my arms.

Fuck, I was gonna come.

I tangled her hair in my fist and dragged her lips to mine, kissing her hard, swallowing her moans. But I had to stop, or I was gonna spill inside of her with no condom. So I pulled out and moved her off of me, still on her stomach. "Stay there," I ordered. With one hand on her back to hold her still, I opened the drawer of the nightstand and grabbed another condom and rolled it on, then got on my knees behind her.

God, that ass. "Get on your hands and knees." I punctuated the order with a slap to one round cheek, loving the sound of her hiss of pain, then slid my fingers between her folds, spreading her moisture. Grabbing her hips, I helped her get into position. "I love the way you look like this, *amore*."

She moaned again as I pushed deep inside of her, and I squeezed her ass in encouragement. "Let me hear you," I told her as I slid slowly in and out.

"No." Glancing back over her shoulder, the smoldering look she gave me didn't match her cold tone.

I narrowed my eyes. This woman was going to drive me insane in the best fucking way. And as I rubbed my palms over her ass and thighs, I pulled out and pushed back in. Then again. And again. Slow and steady. "You're so fucking beautiful," I told her. Because it was the truth. I'd never been with a woman before who was so perfectly made for me. Her skin was a few shades lighter than mine, smooth and soft, especially on the parts I most liked to touch. Her tits. Her ass. The insides of her thighs. Hell, I even loved the way she smelled. Everywhere.

The base of my cock began to tingle, and I increased my pace, moaning as the muscles in her pussy squeezed me tight. "Touch yourself," I told her. "I want you to come with me." For a moment I didn't think she was going to do it, but then she slid her right hand under her body and widened her legs. "That's it, *amore*. Come with me."

At her moaned response, I let go of what little restraint I'd managed to hang onto and started pounding into her, my fingers digging into her hips, keeping her in place. "I'm coming, Veda. Ah, god! I'm coming!" I felt her buck against me right as my orgasm hit me so hard I fell forward, catching myself on one arm so I didn't crush her as my hips spasmed against her ass. And when it was over, I didn't pull out, but stayed inside of her as we fell to the bed and rolled to our sides.

And as I lay there, catching my breath with my face in her fragrant hair, I felt something flutter inside my chest. Something I hadn't felt in a long, long time. A flicker of affection for the woman in my arms.

This had to stop. What the fuck was wrong with me? I'd been with plenty of women since Maria, whores and innocents both, and not one had ever affected me any farther than the length of time it took me to get off. So what was it about this one? Was it because she challenged me? Played hard to get? Or was it because I was actually starting to think of her as mine?

Self-loathing rolled through me, followed by a grim determination. Like a puzzle clicking into place, I hardened my heart, piece by broken piece, forming a wall she'd never be able to breach, locking her out.

Working my arm out from underneath her head, I pulled out of her, still semi-hard, and got to my feet, leaving her lying naked on the bed. Carefully pulling off the condom, I dropped it into the trashcan and found my clothes. I got dressed, ignoring Veda when she sat up and stared at me in confusion.

When I was about to walk out, I stopped, turned, and met her gaze with a cold glare of my own. "Feel free to enjoy the house today. I'll have Lisa move your things back into my room." I paused. Damn it. I should leave her here, and I should leave her alone. But that wasn't going to happen. "I expect to see you at dinner at six sharp. If you're not there, I'll come find you and drag your ass to the table and tie you to the fucking chair." And then I walked out of the room, closing the door just in time to hear something smash against it. The lamp, if I were to guess.

Back in my room, I got in the shower. I washed myself briskly, using the foggy mirror to shave. I would have Lisa arrange for the shopper to come here and get Veda some more clothes. Also, a hairstylist. I hated to do it, but her hair was too natural. It needed to be lightened to match her sister's. The length could be explained by hair extensions, for I absolutely refused to cut it. And contacts. She needed blue contacts. I made a mental note to pass all of that on to Lisa. I had a phone call in an hour and then I had to leave to go check in at the clubs before they opened. My contact with the cartel was meeting me at two to discuss our next shipment.

It had taken a lot of effort on my part to get my father to allow me to keep my position in our business after what I'd "allowed" Mario to do. If some of my cousins had had their way about it, I would've been shipped back to Italy to be "toughened up." The result of which I knew well. I wouldn't have come back. So, after much discussion, I was allowed to stay here in Austin, but only on the condition that my father sent his two best guys down from New York to help me get things back in order.

They were with me for three fucking years. And in all that time, I didn't make one fucking mistake. Not one misstep. However, the feds had made Mario disappear, and they'd done it so well I couldn't find one whisper of where he could be, no matter who I tortured or how many people I paid off. I had nothing on him. No way to hurt him.

At least not until recently, when his new girlfriend said his name to the press. Satisfied that I hadn't lost my edge after the murder of the woman I loved, or maybe because of it, my father finally called off his watch dogs. However, he still insisted I check in with him often.

Taking my cell from my pocket, I tapped my father's name and began to fill him in on where I was with my plan, leaving out the things he didn't need to know. He offered up nothing about what he planned to do with me once my game was done, but that didn't surprise me. Whatever he decided, I would just have to live with it, and be glad he was at least giving me this chance to avenge the woman I'd loved. For me, and for our relationship with the cartel.

An hour later, Tristan and Enzo came into my office when I called them. I was on the phone with one of the managers of my clubs and held up my hand for them to wait where they were while I finished up. "I'll be there in one hour. Have everything ready." Ending the call, I motioned for them to come forward.

Enzo took off his sunglasses. "Do you need me to come with you?"

I shook my head. "No. I want you to stay here with Veda. Tristan, you too. I want eyes on her at all times, either on camera or in person. If one of you has to take a piss, I want the other one watching her every move. Make sure she stays inside the house. I don't want her wandering the grounds." She was angry at me, and I wouldn't put it past her to choose today to try to escape.

"What about security for you?"

"I'll take a couple of the other guys with me." I looked up to find the two of them exchanging an uneasy look. "What?"

It was Tristan who spoke up. "I would feel better...*we* would feel better," he corrected with a glance at Enzo, "if at least one of us was with you."

"So would I," I told them both honestly. "However, you two are the only ones who know about Veda being here.

Because you're the only ones I trust. And I'll be fine," I reassured them. "I'm only going to check on the clubs. Just the normal routine."

"I don't like it," Enzo said. "We've been hearing that Mario's men have been on the move. Stuff not in their normal routine. I don't know what they're doing, but it can't be good."

"They're probably just figuring out that his beloved fiancée has come back from the dead." I stood and pulled on my suit jacket, sticking my cell into the inside pocket. Today I was the businessman, dressed all in black ala Johnny Cash. "Speaking of which, have either of you heard from Rene? Has everything been taken care of?"

"Like she'd never fucking been there," Tristan said. "All records of Nicole's visit to Mexico have been wiped clean."

I nodded. "Good."

They followed me as I walked out of the office and across the main room to the front door. "Remember," I told them as I opened the door, "eyes at all times."

"She'll be here safe and sound when you get back," Tristan assured me.

With a nod, I closed the door behind me and called for one of my men to get the car. I hung up, waiting, and then I pulled my phone out again. "Tony, bring two more guys with you...Yeah...Thank you." Something felt off to me today. I didn't know why. Call it a hunch.

And maybe it was nothing, but it didn't hurt to be cautious.

While I waited for the car to come around, I told Lisa what I needed her to do. She assured me she would take care of everything while I was gone.

The car pulled up, and I got in. As we left the house, my eyes swept the area and I double-checked my weapons. I may have been overreacting, but something was going to go down today. I could feel it in my bones.

CHAPTER 19
LUCA

We made good time getting to the first club, a rundown building on the east side. And I was in and out in forty-five minutes with the cash from the night before and my meeting with my contact from the cartel done. Normally, I didn't make the money runs myself. I'd just send a few of my guys. But once in a while I came myself, just to show my face, or when I needed to set up a shipment. They never knew when those times would be, and I changed up my routine often. Sometimes I was there twice a week, then I wouldn't show for a month and counted on my men to keep me informed about what was going on. I checked in with the management, heard any complaints from the girls when they felt they weren't getting the attention they wanted, and then I was out. Keeping to a routine only tipped off your enemies where you would be and when. I avoided it at all costs.

By four o'clock, I was walking into the last club, buttoning my jacket as I went. Two guys walked behind me. The other was sitting in the SUV, engine running and gun out, guarding the money we'd already collected.

One of my buttons popped off my jacket as I tried to secure it and bounced off the concrete, landing about three feet away to my left. Stepping to the side, I bent down to grab it, and felt searing fire burn a path through the outside of my right shoulder.

"Boss is hit! Boss is hit!"

I saw my man Tony yelling into the phone and heard the screech of tires. Someone grabbed me under the arms and hustled me into the club as shots broke out behind me.

"Down! Down! Everybody down!" Tony yelled as he got me inside and slammed and locked the door. Girls screamed, jumping off whatever customer they'd been grinding on and running awkwardly to the back of the club in their platform shoes, leaving their sugar daddies to duck under the tables and behind the bar.

I pulled my gun from its shoulder holster and took up a spot near the front door, wishing I could see out, but for obvious reasons, there were no windows anywhere in the club. "Motherfucker! Who is that?" I yelled, not taking my eyes from the closed door. "Who the fuck is that?"

No one answered me. But I hadn't really expected them to, because no one fucking knew any better than I did.

Tony and I waited in silence. My shoulder burned like a motherfucker, but I'd taken much worse.

"You okay?" Tony asked.

"Yeah. Feels like it went right through."

A few seconds later, there was banging on the door. Tony opened it and let my other guy inside. "Whoever it was, they're gone."

"The money?" I asked.

He just shook his head. "Didn't even try to go after it."

"That means they were after you, Luca," Tony said.

Sure as fuck they were. I paced away, thinking furiously. Mario was behind this. There was no doubt in my mind. Apparently, my little shopping trip with "Nicole" had done exactly what I wanted it to and word had gotten back to him.

"We should look at your arm, boss."

"It's fine. Call the car back. I need to get the hell out of here."

It was just like Mario to try this kind of shit. He didn't have the balls to face me himself. He just sat behind his desk, safe in the security of wherever the hell he was hiding out, and barked out orders to all his little fucking minions.

While I waited for the car, I settled things with the manager of the club and reassured the girls that they were safe. Most of the customers hightailed it out of there as soon as they heard they could leave, but I wasn't worried about the lost business. They'd be back. The men who frequented these types of places on a daily basis did so for a reason. And gunshots weren't that uncommon in this part of the city. I'd be surprised if anyone had even bothered to call the police, considering how fast it had happened. And the shooter had used a suppressor. Unless someone had seen him, the odds that the shots were heard above the usual city noise were minimal.

By the time I got back to the house, I was starting to feel a little woozy from the loss of blood. It dripped onto the marble floors as I pulled off my jacket and loosened my tie with my left hand.

"Oh, my god! What happened?"

I turned my head to find Veda coming out of the kitchen. The mouth-watering scent of a roast wafted out behind her. Hearing the urgency in her tone, Lisa rushed out, wiping her hands on a towel.

"I'm fine," I told them both, already heading to my office. "Where's Enzo and Tristan?"

"Here." Enzo stepped out from where he'd been standing near the stairs.

"And here," Tristan said from behind me.

Without a word, they followed me and Tony to my office. I poured myself a glass of whiskey with my good hand to ease the throbbing in my shoulder while Tony filled them in.

"It had to be Mario," Enzo said. "Or is there someone else gunning for you we don't know about?"

I downed my drink in two swallows and poured myself another. "Not that I'm aware of."

"What are we gonna do about it?" Tristan asked.

"Nothing," I told him.

"How can we do nothing? He tried to kill you."

Yes, he did. If I hadn't popped off that button, I'd still be lying in that dirty parking lot next to the trash and hypodermic needles. Before I could say anything else, I heard a scuffle outside the door.

"You can't go in there, Veda! Wait...no...wait! Dammit!"

The door flew open and Veda flew into the room, skidding to a halt when we all turned to look at her. She looked around a bit nervously at first, and then her gray eyes landed on me. She took a step forward, then stopped, her bravado leaving her under the weight of our stares.

I tilted my head, running my eyes over her. She was wearing a pair of washed-out jean shorts and a T-shirt with a Rolling Stones logo. Her feet were bare, and her hair was pulled back in a high ponytail. "Veda, this is Tony. Tony, Veda."

"Holy shit," he mumbled, more to himself than to any of us. Then he turned to me, eyebrows lowered in confusion. "Wait. Is this Mario's girlfriend?"

"Fiancée," I corrected. "And no, it's her twin sister. But close enough, don't you think?"

"Spitting image," he said, looking toward her again. His dark eyes roved over her, from the top of her head to her bare toes and back again, lingering on her legs and tits.

My upper lip lifted, baring my teeth. "Put your eyes back in your fucking head and get the fuck out," I told him. Then I waved my hand toward the door. "All of you. Get out."

"Luca," Enzo said. "We need to talk about Mario."

"There's nothing to discuss. This is exactly what I wanted to happen." I glanced down at the trail of blood darkening my shirt. "Well, not the fucking getting shot part—"

"You were shot?" Veda paled, her eyes zeroing in on the arm I held protectively against my body. She shoved Tristan out of the way and took three more steps toward me before she stopped again, unsure of her place.

He glanced down at her, one eyebrow lifted in surprise.

"Out," I said again.

"Your arm," Tristan said. "We need to call the doc."

"Veda will take care of my arm. Go." I swung my whiskey glass in the direction of the door. With a nod, Enzo turned and walked out of the office. Tony followed, and Tristan smiled at Veda as he passed her, then closed the door behind him. She didn't even glance up at him.

When they were gone, I collapsed against my chair, spilling whiskey all over my shirt and pants.

"Oh shit," Veda said. When I raised my chin, she was in front of me, unbuttoning my shirt.

I grabbed her wrist, wincing. "It's fine."

"It's not fucking fine," she practically yelled at me. "You're too pale, your skin is cold, and you almost passed out just now. So let go of my arm."

After a pause, I did as she asked. "It went right through," I told her. "And I didn't almost pass out. I'm just fucking tired."

She ignored that last part. Either she believed me, or she just didn't want to argue with me. "Are you sure it went through?"

"I think I've been shot enough times to know the difference."

Her fingers froze on the buttons for a moment, and then her eyes dropped to the expanse of chest she'd just revealed, searching for evidence.

"Here," I told her, pulling my shirt aside to reveal a faint round scar near my left hip. "It made a bigger hole coming out the back, which is probably why you didn't notice it." I tried to smile at her look of horror, but it turned into a grimace as a wave of pain reverberated down my arm. "There's another one in my right thigh. That one got stuck," I told her. "And the doc had to dig it out."

"Is that it?" she asked quietly.

I thought about her question. My memories were getting fuzzy. "I'm missing a part of my left ear. Just barely. But if you look close, you'll see where the bullet grazed me."

Her eyes flew to that ear. "Good god," she whispered.

I watched the horror flit across her face. "I can street fight with the best of them. But even I can't outrun a bullet."

Silently, she helped me get my shirt off. I tried not to make any noise, but I couldn't contain the hiss of pain when she peeled the wet material away from the wound, already beginning to clot. Standing up, she leaned over me to check the back.

Soft strands of her hair tickled my face. I tucked my face into the curve of her neck and shoulder, inhaling her clean scent. It smelled like home to me. And then I laughed to myself. Maybe she was right, and I'd lost more blood than I thought.

"Looks like you're right. I think it went right through." She straightened up, wringing her hands, and I carefully eased back against my chair. "I don't know what to do, Luca. Do you have a first aid kit or something?"

"Ask Lisa," I told her. "She knows where it is." My eyes dropped to her ass as she rushed out to do as I'd said, a bit surprised at her eagerness to help me.

She was back in record time, a first aid kit in one hand and a bowl of water in the other. Her hands shook as she balanced it on her hip and shoved aside some papers on my desk before she set everything down. She eyed my shoulder for a few seconds, then turned and ran back out of the office, returning with some washcloths and one large towel. "I thought it would help protect your chair."

"The blood will wipe off," I told her.

She made me lean forward and shoved it behind me anyway. Picking up one of the washcloths, she dipped it in the bowl of water. "And you know this, do you?"

"As a matter of fact, I do. Why do you think there's no carpet in this house?"

Her gray eyes flashed up to mine, but only for a second before she went back to her task. Carefully, she wiped the blood from my arm and hand as I sipped on my whiskey and tried to ignore how good she smelled.

While she worked, I let my eyes travel over the top of her hair. It was lighter than it was this morning. I wasn't sure I liked this color. It looked cheap. The same as half of the girls at my clubs. And it was missing the soft, subtle tones of glinting sunlight that she had naturally. "Your hair is different."

Something about my tone of voice made her pause. She didn't comment, she only swallowed and went back to work on the bullet hole in my shoulder. When the blood was all wiped away, she dropped the dirty cloth in the bowl of water and picked up the bottle of alcohol. It seemed she knew at least a little about treating wounds. She paused, her eyes going from my shoulder to my face.

"Just do it," I told her.

"This is going to hurt," she warned me, and I almost laughed. I was very familiar with the feeling of an antiseptic being poured into an open wound, whether straight up alcohol or vodka, it all burned the same.

Veda leaned over me, the bottle raised in her hand, then she paused, grabbed the towel, and held it against my chest and arm.

I gulped down the last of my whiskey but hung on to my glass, bracing myself. Seconds ticked by... "For fuck's sake, Veda! Just do it!"

She jumped, liquid splashing onto the bullet wound, and I clenched my jaw, breathing through my nose. Her eyes darted to my face, and then she tipped the bottle, pouring more alcohol into the open wound.

"Son of a fuckin' bitch!" I clamped my teeth together, bearing the pain as spears of fire radiated out from the bullet hole and ricocheted down my arm and up into my neck.

"I'm sorry," she whispered as she patted the towel around the edges.

"You have to do the back, too," I told her.

Veda nodded. "Okay."

I leaned forward in the chair to give her better access. This time she didn't hesitate, and I managed to keep my mouth shut, though I couldn't contain the hiss of pain that escaped.

"Okay. Now what?" she asked. "A bandage? Do you need some ointment or anything?"

"Is the back still bleeding?" I asked her.

She peeked around my arm and grabbed a rag. "Yeah. A little." I felt her looking at me and glanced up to find her gray eyes dark with worry. "Luca, you need a doctor. What if something was damaged? An artery or nerves or something?"

"If an artery was damaged, I would've been dead before we left the club," I told her.

Opening the first aid kit, she grabbed some bandages. "I'm going to cover up the wounds so nothing gets in them and then I'm going to go ask Lisa or one of the guys to call your doctor. I assume you have someone who makes house calls?"

I grunted as she slapped a bandage on the wound in the back and pressed down. "You watch too many bad movies."

"Okay, then. Hospital it is."

"I'm not going to the fucking hospital."

She didn't argue with me, just finished bandaging me up. It made me suspicious, but for once, I couldn't read her.

I watched her clean up everything off my desk. Towel under her arm, she picked up the bowl of bloody water and took it out of my office.

Getting up, I stood where I was for a second to make sure I wasn't going to face plant, then made my way over to the bottle of whiskey and poured myself another drink. I drank half of it, filled my glass again, and went back to my chair.

Veda walked back into my office. "The doc is on his way," she told me casually.

"I don't need a fucking doctor," I grumbled.

She stopped and turned. "You wanna take me to your party, Luca? Show me off? Have a few drinks...maybe fuck me afterward?"

My cock jumped to attention. Apparently, I hadn't lost that much blood. Tilting my head, I sent her a questioning look.

"Let the doctor look at your fucking arm," she ordered in no uncertain terms, then she marched out of the room.

I grinned like a loon when she slammed the door.

I'd definitely lost too much blood.

CHAPTER 20
VEDA

I stared at myself in the full-length mirror in my room. With Luca wounded, I'd managed to argue my way into keeping my own room for a few more days, at least, so I didn't accidentally hurt him. I thought I needed the alone time, but after the first night, it became very apparent to me that...yeah, not so much. However, I wasn't about to tell *him* that.

I smoothed down the skirt of the blush pink dress he'd bought me.

No. Scratch that. The dress he'd bought *Nicole*. The material was soft and breezy, and it hugged my curves perfectly. My eyes traveled from the top of my newly highlighted hair to my blue eyes (thanks to some really uncomfortable contacts) to my painted pink toes. I had a feeling of disembodiment as I looked at the woman reflected back to me.

I wasn't me anymore. The woman staring back at me with emotionless eyes didn't just look like Nicole, she *was* her.

The bedroom door opened, and Luca came in. Tearing my eyes away from the image of my dead sister, I looked over at him, and immediately wished I hadn't.

He was dressed in a double-breasted, dark navy suit with a subtle plaid print of a slightly lighter blue. The shirt beneath it was black, as were his loafers and the sling holding his right arm close to his body to minimize any jostling of his shoulder. No tie. Nothing flashy. But he didn't need it. This man was devastating in nothing but a pair of gym shorts.

"You look lovely," he told me with an odd tone in his voice.

"I look like her," I responded, and I wondered if my eyes were as dead as my voice when he looked into them.

Luca said nothing at first. Then he held out his uninjured arm. "Shall we?"

Walking over to my shoes where I'd left them by the bed, I slipped my feet into them, bending over to adjust the straps. The heels were higher than anything I would ever normally wear, and I prayed that if nothing else, I wouldn't fall and make an ass of myself tonight.

I was feeling comfortably numb as he escorted me out of the room, down the stairs, and out to the waiting car. Ever the gentlemen, he helped me in, then walked around the front of the car to get in on the other side. I watched him through the windshield. If he was nervous about taking me out as Nicole for the first time, he didn't show it.

And so, the game began.

"Where are we going exactly?" I asked him once he was beside me in the backseat.

"My uncle is turning ninety-years-old tonight. In"—he looked at his watch—"precisely one hour and seventeen minutes."

"You know what time he was born?"

"Only because he started telling everyone from the day he turned seventy. He was convinced he wouldn't live long enough to see his birthday party, and kept trying to get us to move the time up."

I smiled, forgetting for a moment why I was there. "He sounds like a piece of work."

Luca laughed softly. A real laugh. With little lines creasing the skin around his eyes. I caught my breath as I stared at him.

He was beautiful. And dangerous. And he made me feel alive, despite the fact I was a walking dead woman.

"He is," he told me. "He's also my favorite uncle." He looked over at me, and his blue eyes were warm, yet chills scuttled across my skin to be on the receiving end of that look. A rare occurrence. "He's going to love you."

"Me? Or Nicole?"

He huffed out a little laugh. "I don't think he would've liked your sister much, from what you've told me."

"Unfortunately, I won't be able to act like my normal, charming self if we're going to pull this off."

He frowned. "Why wouldn't you? I happen to like your normal, charming self."

He did? "Um, I just figured people would be there who knew Nicole. They would know right away I wasn't her from the difference between us."

"Only my family will be there. No one who would've known her since she met my brother after he exiled himself."

"Oh." Then what was the point of getting me dressed up like her?

As if he'd read my mind, Luca answered my question. "I believe Mario has his men watching me at all times. Where I go. What I do. And with who. They won't get close enough to notice any differences between your personality and Nicole's. However, they *will* run right back to him to tell him what they saw."

Ah. I looked out the window, a little unsettled by what he'd told me.

"What is it, *amore?*"

If I didn't know better, I would think he was truly concerned. "Nothing," I told him. I wasn't sure I could explain the feelings coursing through me, even if I wanted to.

He clasped my chin in his fingers and forcefully turned my face toward him, his eyes searching mine. Looking for...what? "Veda, tell me what's on your mind." Although the words were spoken quietly, I didn't miss the undertone of dominance. He wasn't going to let this go.

I pulled my face from his grip to look down at my hands, twisted in my lap, as I tried to get my thoughts together.

"Dammit, what the hell is it?" he asked again.

"Won't they come after you again?" I glanced at him from the corner of my eye, then looked back out the window. I didn't want him to see the concern on my face, misplaced as it was. What did I care if they finished the job next time they came after him? If they could manage not to fuck things up again, I would be free.

Instead of the sensation of euphoria I expected to feel when I imagined him gone forever from my life, a wave of sorrow crashed over me, hitting me so hard I had to catch my breath before I drowned.

Luca took my hand, and when I looked over at him, I could swear I saw the same struggle within him. "That's what I'm counting on," he told me. "But don't worry, they won't get so close to me next time."

"I'm not worried," I lied.

He searched my face, and then one side of his mouth lifted in a knowing smirk. I pulled my hand from his and returned it to my lap, then turned back to the window.

We rode in silence the rest of the way, only the soft notes of a piano coming over the car's speakers to break the tension between us.

What seemed like forever but was probably only a few minutes later, Enzo rolled down the privacy glass. "We'll be there in two minutes, Luca."

Reaching inside his jacket, Luca pulled out his Glock and checked that it was ready to go before he slid it back into the holster. "Pull up as close to the front door of the restaurant as you can get," he told him. "I'll slide out Veda's side." To me he said, "When Enzo stops the car, get out, but stay behind the door until I'm with you. Understand?"

Oh, I understood all right. "If it's not safe for us, why are we here?"

He must've heard the thread of panic in my voice, for he brought his eyes back around to mine. "Nothing will happen to you."

Tonight. I heard the unspoken word, even though he didn't say it. He didn't have to.

He reached out for my hand, but I pulled it away.

"Veda. I won't let anything happen to you, *amore*. Just do exactly as I say until we get inside, understand?"

I nodded and tried to calm my racing heart.

"I'm not expecting any trouble, but it never hurts to be prepared."

Again, I nodded. What else was I supposed to do?

We pulled up to a small cottage that looked like it had been lifted right out of the Irish countryside. White with green trim, I half expected to see fairies flitting about the gardens out front. Or a hobbit with furry feet to walk out the little wooden door. I went to reach for the door handle, but Luca stopped me with a hand on my arm. "Hang on, Veda."

Enzo had his phone to his ear. After a few seconds, he gave the go-ahead.

"I'll be right behind you," Luca told me.

I opened the door and slid out, wobbling a bit on my heels before stepping aside just enough to give Luca room to get out. I may have been there against my will, but I wasn't stupid. I didn't want to get shot. Enzo came around the back of the car, and after a quick look around, the three of us walked swiftly to the entrance.

Enzo opened the door, blocking us with his body, and we were greeted with raucous laughter as we walked into a small foyer that was littered with photos of previous guests and an old-fashioned sign-in book. Beyond the foyer, there were three small rooms that branched off the center of the cottage, and each room had just enough tables to fill the space, but still give the patrons a sense of privacy. Old-fashioned wallpaper covered the walls, white with little green flowers. White lace tablecloths covered each table, and there were real candles in the center. Not the fake kind with the electric bulbs made to look like them. The laughter I'd heard upon entering came from the very back. And from the portion of that room I could see, there were people packed inside, wall to wall.

"I'm going to park the car and I'll be right back," Enzo told Luca just as a lovely woman with long, straight, dark hair, pink lipstick that didn't match her coloring, and a modest flowery dress came to greet us.

"Welcome! Welcome!" she said. Her voice was hushed and had a lilting Irish accent. Up close, I could see she was older than she'd first appeared. Probably in her late forties, at least. "How are you, Luca?"

"I'm fine, Marg. Thank you. How are you and the family?"

"Oh, we're well. Thank you so much for asking." She smiled at me and picked up a couple of menus, then led us to the back room.

There was an uproar of greetings as we entered the space, and I immediately spotted the birthday boy sitting at the head of a long table with a cigar in his mouth and a crown on his head. And not like a paper crown that you buy at a party store, but one that appeared to be pure gold with different colored stones at the tip of each peak.

If I were a betting girl, I would put my money on that thing being actual real gold and gemstones.

The man wearing it had skin like leather and a sunken mouth, but when he spotted Luca, he smiled wide, revealing a lack of teeth. It transformed his face, his cloudy eyes sparkling as he tried to get up without upsetting his crown. "Come here, boy!" he yelled in a strong Italian accent.

Taking my hand, Luca made his way through the crowd of people to greet his uncle. "*Ciao, zio.* How are you?" Still holding my hand, he kissed him on both cheeks.

"I might actually make it to my birthday," the man exclaimed. Then his watery eyes landed on me. "And who is this *bella ragazza?*"

"This *pretty girl,*" Luca translated for me with a wink, "is Nicole." The name slid naturally from his lips. "*Amore,* meet my favorite uncle."

The elderly man took both of my hands in his and kissed my knuckles. "Ah, it's so nice to meet you, Nicole," he told me. "I'm Aldo."

"Thank you for letting me crash your party," I told him.

"Did you bring me a gift?" he asked.

I pressed my lips together and shook my head. "No. Sorry." And I really was. "Luca didn't give me a chance to go shopping."

He waved his hand toward his nephew with a "Pfft. Of course he didn't. If he's smart, he won't let you out of his sight."

Oh, if you only knew.

"You come sit here by me," he told me. "I'm the most interesting person at this party anyway."

"Now *that* I believe," I told him sincerely.

As I took my chair, Luca leaned down and told me, "I'm going to leave you in my uncle's trusted hands for a moment. I'll be right back." Then, putting his mouth right against my ear, he said, "Remember where you are. These are not the people who will save you."

Icy fingers trailed down my spine as Luca walked away. I watched him touch the sleeve of another man—quite a bit shorter than Luca and with darker hair—then lean in to say something. The man nodded and excused himself from the lady—and I mean that loosely—he was with. The other women there were giving her just as much side-eye as I was. I guess even mobsters had *some* standards. With a last glance in my direction, Luca followed the other man and the two of them went out a side door.

I felt Luca's uncle pat my hand. "Don't you worry, Luca has some business to discuss with my other nephew, and then he'll be right back. Until then, you're safe here with me. We'll order some drinks, and you can tell me all about yourself." He waved to the waiter who'd just appeared at the table and was taking more drink orders.

"I'd much rather hear about you," I told him. And I meant it. Looking like my sister was one thing. I'd dealt with that my entire life. Pretending to be anything more...I wasn't sure I could do it without bursting into tears. For her. And for me.

He ordered us some wine, and then with a wink, he said, "I'll tell you about my boyhood growing up in Italy."

"I would really love that," I said in all honesty. And I settled in to hear his stories.

CHAPTER 21
LUCA

My conversation with my cousin took longer than I'd expected. Mark was having some issues with another member of the family. One who didn't think Mark should be in the position he'd attained after his brother was killed last year, and he wanted to know if we all thought that way. I assured him I had nothing but respect for the way he'd been handling things. The one who was giving him a hard time, on the other hand...

"Gio is an asshole," I told him. "I don't know how he grew up the way he did."

"He says he can't trust me."

Personally, I trusted Mark way more than Gio. If I didn't, he wouldn't be taking care of the money collections for me at the clubs. Just for the time being, so as to make me less of a target. "How is business going?"

"Good, for the most part." He relayed some of the issues one of the managers was having with a couple of the girls.

"If you want my opinion," Mark told me. "I think you should get rid of those two and bring in some new blood. Hopefully younger and without the tracks on their arms."

"The patrons don't care if they still have the needles stuck in them, as long as they get ass and tits in their faces."

"And in their hands." His mouth twisted in disgust as he said it.

I shrugged. "If that's what the girls want, who am I to stop them from making money?"

We were standing outside the connected kitchen, and when we saw the food coming out, we wrapped up our conversation and headed back inside just as everyone was finding their seats. "Where is...Nicole?" I asked my uncle when I got to his side. Jesus fucking Christ. I hoped that stutter was minor enough he didn't catch on, but luckily, he was more interested in the lamb the waiter was carving for him tableside.

"She went to the ladies' room a little bit ago. Maybe you should go check on her. She's been gone for a while." He winked at me and picked up his fork as another waiter placed his salad in front of him.

I glanced around the table. Everyone was there except for Gio, the cousin Mark was having issues with. An uneasy feeling trickled down my spine. "Where's Gio?" I asked my uncle.

He waved his fork in the air. "Eh, who knows with that one? If we're lucky, he left."

The waiter set my salad on the table along with one for Veda. "I'll be right back," I told my uncle. "Save my seat."

I headed toward the restrooms at the front of the cottage. The ladies' room was empty. Turning to the men's room directly opposite, I tried the knob. It was locked.

With a frown, I tried to listen above the Irish jig that played over the speakers placed discreetly in the corners of the ceiling. I wouldn't put it past my little spitfire to make use of whichever one was empty. When I didn't hear anything, I started to turn away...

"You bitch!"

The men's room door flew open, and Veda ran straight at me, her eyes unseeing in her panic to get out, her mouth bleeding and her hair mussed.

I opened my good arm and caught her. "Hey, hey, it's me," I told her when she started to struggle. "It's me."

Pulling back, she looked up at my face, and then threw herself back against my chest and wrapped her arms around my waist. She shook like a leaf in my arms, and I could feel her heart pounding.

I smoothed down her hair as I stared over her head at Gio, who had come charging out of the bathroom behind her, only to stop short when he saw Veda tucked against me.

"What the fuck did you do to her?" My voice was deadly quiet, in contrast to the rage that was rising inside of me, screaming at me to pound him into the ground first and ask questions later.

"Who the fuck *is* this bitch?" he sneered, his teeth red with blood.

"Go back to the table," I told Veda without taking my eyes from him. "Have some dinner."

"Luca, no. It's okay. I'm fine."

My eyes never left my cousin. "Do as I say."

But, of course, that was expecting too much. "I'm not going anywhere without you."

Fine. Before either of them knew what I was about, I stepped around her and pulled my Glock. Lifting my right arm still in the sling, I didn't even feel the pain as I shoved Gio against the wall with my forearm against his throat. Pressing the muzzle of the gun to his temple, I gave him a little time to confess. "Do you have anything to tell me now?"

"Luca! What are you doing?" Veda cried. But my girl was smart. She didn't try to pull me off of him.

"Did he touch you?" I asked her calmly without taking my eyes from my scumbag cousin.

"I didn't do anything." Pink spittle ran down Gio's chin and soaked into my sling. "Now let me go, you fucking prick."

I pushed the nozzle of the gun harder against his skull, my finger resting lightly on the trigger.

"Fucking hell, Luca!" he raged at me, his face a mottled red.

"Did he touch you, *amore*?" I repeated. The thought of this asshole's hands on Veda sent me spiraling into a rage such as I'd never experienced before. Not even when Maria had died. My gun hand shook. "DID HE TOUCH YOU?"

"Yes," she yelled back. "But I handled it, Luca! Now stop it before you shoot him!"

"Oh, I plan to shoot him," I told her. "I just want him to piss himself a little first."

"Luca, please."

"What the fuck is going on back here?"

I didn't turn to see who had asked. I didn't have to. If I knew my family, and I did, the entire party would be crowded behind Veda to watch what was going down. Witnesses were important.

"Luca, Luca," my uncle called my name as he had since I was a boy. "Put down the gun. You can't go splattering your cousin's brains all over the wall. Think of the cleaning bill."

"I will personally see to it myself," I told him without taking my eyes from Gio. "It will be like it never happened." Sweat began to bead at his temple, and although he tried to keep up the tough guy act, his eyes swung over to our uncle, silently pleading with him to save him.

"Luca, please," Veda whispered behind me. "I don't want any bloodshed."

"This *stronzo* should've thought about that before he put his hands on something that's MINE."

"I didn't know who the fuck she was!" Gio shouted. "Jesus Christ, Luca."

"So, what? You think any of us would bring a woman to our uncle's birthday, a family event, and that we wouldn't care if you fucking raped her in the men's room?"

"I wasn't gonna rape her, man!"

I pushed the nozzle of the gun harder into his temple. "Then what, exactly, were you doing to her in there? Why does she have blood on her mouth?"

"Because the bitch fucking bit me! That's why!" Spittle hit my face and ran down my cheek.

"Luca..." My uncle slowly made his way toward me until he was standing right next to the two of us. Pulling out a handkerchief, he wiped off my face as I debated whether or not to kill my cousin. "Don't ruin my birthday by killing family at my dinner. It might be my last celebration. If, tomorrow, you still feel that you need to avenge your lady's honor," he shrugged, "you can kill him then."

Gio turned wide eyes to him. "What the fuck, *Zio?*"

But our uncle just took a step back and raised both arms out to the side with another shrug. "What? You bring this shit on yourself, Giovanni."

Rage still boiled inside of me, heating my blood and making my trigger finger itchy. But my uncle was right. I couldn't splatter Gio's brains all over the wall at his birthday dinner. It was disrespectful. If my father was here, he would never allow it. Pressing my arm a little harder against his throat, I enjoyed the way he gagged, fighting for a breath. "I think you need to suddenly go home. I don't think you're feeling very well."

He tried to nod.

With one last shove, I stepped back. "Pack up his dinner, please," I told our hostess.

"Oh, of course. Right away." With a nervous smile, she scuttled off to do as I asked.

Coughing and gagging, Gio stumbled out of the alcove we'd been standing in. One hand on his throat and the other shoving people out of the way, he ran out the front door.

Turning on my heel, I made to follow him, my eyes on the front door as everyone wandered back to their food. I needed some fucking air.

Veda grabbed my jacket as I passed. "Where are you going?"

I didn't stop. I had to get the hell out of there and make sure that motherfucker left before I changed my mind.

Gun still in my hand, I pushed open the front door and walked into the night just as Gio's god awful yellow sports car spun out of the drive, cutting off another car in his haste. I spotted Enzo parked on the right side of the dirt lot. When he saw me, he got of the car, but didn't come any closer. I indicated for him to stay where he was and he gave me a nod, making himself comfortable against the back of the SUV where he could keep an eye on me while still giving me my privacy.

Gravel crunched behind me, and through the ringing in my ears, I heard Veda cursing under her breath about the "goddamn death traps" she had to wear.

"You shouldn't be out here," I told her. "It might not be safe."

"Neither should you," she retorted, picking her way carefully over to me. "How's your shoulder?"

I'd forgotten about it, honestly. Probably the adrenaline still rushing through my bloodstream. "It's fine." I turned to look at her. "Are you hurt?" I swear to god, if that asshole had left so much as a tiny bruise on her...

She shook her head. "No. Not really."

My fingers tightened around my gun. "Not really?"

"I'm fine. I just need a drink."

I watched her as she wiped the blood from her mouth with a napkin she'd brought outside and fixed her dress. "Why did he think he could fuck you, *Nicole?*"

Slowly, she looked up at me. "That's not my name," she whispered.

"It is while you're here. Now answer my fucking question."

Her mouth, now cleaned of blood, twisted in anger and disgust. Without a word, she turned to go back inside.

Shoving my gun into its holster, I grabbed her arm before she could get far. "Answer my fucking question."

"Fuck you." She practically spit the words at me.

"Were you flirting with him?" Just the thought of her smiling at another man made me want to tear apart every room in this house, piece by piece.

"Let go of my arm."

"Tell me what happened," I insisted.

"Why?" she cried. Her eyes blazed with anger behind the fake blue. "So you can blame me because that dude can't keep his dick in his pants? Fuck that."

I yanked her toward me, and she stumbled, landing hard against my chest. My own dick was swollen and hard. I needed to be inside of her. To claim her. Make her remember just who the fuck she belonged to. The urge was overwhelming, even though I knew it made no sense. Wrapping my fist in her hair, I pulled her head back until she had to look down her nose to see me. "You are mine, Veda," I told her quietly, using her proper name. "It would do you well to remember that."

She glared up at me. "So someone in your family attacks me when I'm just trying to pee, and it's my fault? Is the dress you picked out for me too slutty? Is that it? Maybe the heels you insisted I wear are too high? Hair too blonde? Too much makeup?"

My anger was misplaced. I knew this. But I couldn't contain it. I was angry at my cousin, not at her. And I was angry at myself for giving a shit.

Madness rose inside of me, screaming for release. And since it would be hours until I was home to take it out on my punching bag, that left the woman standing in front of me. *My* woman. With my hand still tangled in her hair, I marched her over to the side of the building where we'd be hidden from prying eyes. She didn't whine. She didn't cry out. She just stomped on over there. Her body tense. Ready to give back as good as she got.

Around us, the night was dark, with only the slightest bit of light coming from a window in the kitchen, a structure that had been added on as a separate piece to the side of the house, and the occasional headlights from a passing car. With the property being on a slight rise from the road and surrounded by trees, no one would see us here. But Enzo would be able to hear me if I needed him.

I leaned into her, pressing her back against the siding with the weight of my body. "Do you feel what you do to me, *vita?*" *My life.* The word slipped out with barely any notice from me. "Do you feel how crazy you make me?" With my hand in her hair to hold her still, she could only press her palm against my chest in a feeble effort to keep me off of her, the bloody napkin still fisted in the other, her eyes staring at nothing over my shoulder. A roar of laughter came from inside the restaurant. But it was muffled by the thick, stone walls, and not loud enough to hide her sharp breaths.

"I did nothing wrong," she bit out.

"Did he kiss you? Hmm?" I nipped at her lips as she tried to tighten them against me. "Did he stick his tongue down your fucking throat?" I licked the seam of her mouth.

She wouldn't look at me. Wouldn't open for me.

"Did you fucking like it?"

Her eyes shot to mine, and I saw a fury there that rivaled my own. I wanted to rip out those contacts and watch the storm brew, and barely contained myself from doing it.

Instead, I tightened my grip on her hair until she winced. "Tell me what he fucking did to you."

"It doesn't matter."

Touching my forehead to hers, I took a deep breath. "But it does, *amore*. It does fucking matter."

"Not to me," she said.

"No?" I asked her.

She tried to shake her head, but my grip was too tight. So she repeated, "No."

With a growl, I lowered my head and caught her mouth with mine, biting her lips until she succumbed to my kiss. Opening her hand, she let the napkin fall to the ground to grip my shirt with both hands, and I felt the struggle inside of her. "Kiss me, *vita*," I begged against her mouth. "Kiss me, *amore*."

CHAPTER 22
VEDA

Luca's big body shuddered against mine when I responded to his plea by running the tip of my tongue along his bottom lip. He was angry at what happened. I got that. So was I. His fucking cousin had come walking into the little alcove where the bathrooms were right as I opened the ladies' room door and wouldn't let me leave. And when I'd gotten tired of dealing with him and tried to knee him in the balls, he'd shoved me into the men's room with him, closing and locking the door behind us.

I told him I was with Luca, and he responded by telling me that his cousin was a pussy and didn't deserve a woman like me. I disagreed, loudly, playing my role to a "T." Then he'd backed me up against the door, much as Luca was doing now, grabbed my jaw, and pressed his slimy lips against my mouth. As I tried to shove him off of me, he managed to get one hand underneath my dress and grabbed me between the legs, squeezing hard until my mouth opened on a cry of pain. Then he stuck his tongue in my mouth.

I bit down until I tasted blood and he released me.

Taking advantage of his surprise, I'd spun around and unlocked the door, throwing myself out of the small room and right into Luca's arms. Where I now found myself again. So, yeah, I totally got the anger. And this man who held me now was no pussy. He was a dominant male. I understood that also. Just like I understood why he was acting the way he was, even if I didn't like it.

Or hell, maybe I did.

I moaned as he took my mouth in a harsh kiss—nothing like the slobbery mess of his cousin—and tried to press closer to him. But his arm in its sling was between us, and I didn't want to hurt him, so I backed off as much as I could.

With a growl of frustration, Luca ripped off his sling and threw it onto the ground. Then took my face between both of his palms and kissed me until my lips were swollen and bruised and bloody from his bites. And even then, he didn't stop, nipping at my jaw and sucking on my throat as his hands fell to my breasts. "Touch me, *amore*," he commanded. "I want to feel your hand on my cock."

I did as he ordered. With shaking hands, I unfastened his pants, his moan in my ear so utterly erotic as I shoved down his boxer briefs and pulled out the long, thick length of him, running my hand up and down, feeling the silken slide of his skin over his rock-hard erection and squeezing the head in my fist. A drop of moisture beaded at the tip as I rubbed my thumb over it.

He cursed beneath his breath as his hands ran down along my sides to my hips, where they stopped. "Take off your panties."

With a nervous look around, I lifted my skirt and hooked my thumbs under the waistband of my underwear, then slid them down over my hips and thighs, letting them fall to the ground at my feet. I kicked them to the side. My heart pounded in my chest as I waited for what he would do next.

"Are you wet for me, Veda?" he murmured in my ear.

I whimpered as he lifted my skirt, exposing my bare flesh to the warm night air. He sucked on my earlobe, playing with the diamond stud there, one hand holding up my skirt and the other gripping my naked hip. With his thumb, he drew slow circles on my skin, closer and closer to my core with every stroke.

"I think you are," he told me. "Shall we find out?"

My hips jerked forward when his thumb brushed over the crease between my legs, finding that *exact* spot with an accuracy that unnerved me. Desperately, I hung onto his shoulders as he pressed his thumb between the folds of my flesh.

"Were you wet for my cousin, Veda? Did you moan for him like this? Did he touch you here?" His blue eyes were dark with fury. "No one touches you here but me, do you understand?" He cupped me in his hand. "This is *mine*."

I didn't bother to answer, and I don't think he was expecting me to. Widening my legs, I gave him better access and was rewarded when he slid one thick finger inside of me.

"Did he make you come? Did you scream his name?"

I shook my head, incapable of speaking as he worked my clit, the heavy weight in my womb building into surges of desire that swelled higher and stronger with every circle of his fingers. My legs trembled as he took me right to the edge, holding me there with a groan until he took pity on me, and I crashed over with his name on my lips. His mouth came down hard on mine, swallowing my cries as my orgasm ripped through me until I was limp and boneless in his arms.

"You are mine, Veda." His voice was little more than a growl as he lifted me against the wall with his hands under my ass. "MINE," he gritted out, the tip of his cock nudging me. "ONLY mine." With one thrust of his hips, he buried himself balls deep inside of me, forcing my body to stretch to accommodate the size of him. But I was ready for him. So ready.

My legs came up to wrap around his waist and my arms twisted around his shoulders as he fucked me against the wall, my face in his neck to muffle the cries I could no longer contain. I wanted this. I wanted him to love me. To care about me. To hate the thought of me with anyone else. But I was quickly becoming the pawn in my own game.

"Say it," he ordered. "Say you are mine."

"I'm yours, Luca," I cried.

His arms tightened painfully, brutally, around me. His breathing loud and harsh in my ear as he pounded into me fast and hard. The siding of the cottage scraped my bare back, but I barely felt it, lost in the sensations he demanded I feel. Just when I was about to beg him to slow down, to stop, to give me a moment, he tensed, his entire body hardening around me, and I felt his release and heard him call my name like a curse just before he hid his face in my hair.

We stayed like that for several long minutes, just holding each other, until gradually, I remembered where we were. "Luca, someone is going to find us."

"Let them," he said. He lifted his head, and although he still wasn't happy, the fire in his eyes had died down to mere embers. Carefully now, he pulled out of me, and I unwound my legs from around his waist.

As I found my feet again, my hands slid over his shoulders and down his arms, pushing off his jacket as I went. There was a wet spot on his shirt. And when I pulled my hand away and put it in the light coming from the kitchen, my palm was bloody. "Luca, you're bleeding!"

He picked up his sling from the ground. "That would explain why my shoulder is throbbing like a bitch."

"Why didn't you say something?"

Looking down at me, one side of his mouth curved up in a devilish smile. "It didn't hurt until just now." When I only stared at him, he sighed. "It'll be fine. I'll clean it up when we get home."

Home. Something twisted inside of me. The lake house wasn't my home. I didn't know if I'd ever see my home again. However, if being with this man would save my life...well, perhaps it wouldn't be such a terrible thing if our fights always ended like this. I found my underwear on the ground and shook the dirt from them, then wadded them up in my hand. I'd throw them away when I got inside.

Luca must've sensed the change in my mood, for he reached out to touch my back. I flinched, releasing a hiss when he touched my skin, scraped raw from the side of the house. His brows lowered into a frown as he turned me around. "Jesus Christ. Why the fuck didn't *you* say anything?"

He was angry again. "Probably the same reason you didn't notice your shoulder was bleeding."

Taking off his coat, he carefully put it over my shoulders. A little awkwardly with one hand, but he managed. "I'll go in and make our excuses."

"But I'm starving," I told him. I really was. I hadn't eaten yet that day. "And it smells so good."

His eyes traveled over my face. "We'll take it to go." He paused, looking like he wanted to say more. But then the mood changed as he seemed to shake off whatever was bothering him. "Enzo!" he called.

Oh, my god. I'd totally forgotten about Enzo standing by the car. My cheeks burned as he came walking around the corner of the house.

"Put Veda in the car. I'm going to get our food to go and tell everyone we're leaving."

"I'll pull up to the door," he told Luca. Then he put his hand on my back and I tried not to wince as he led me over to the car.

I got into the backseat and was glad I had Luca's jacket when it cushioned my back against the leather. Leaning my head against the headrest, I closed my eyes and hoped Enzo couldn't hear the way my stomach was growling.

Luca came out five minutes later with a bag in his hand, his eyes sharp as he took in the area around him and got into the car. "I got you the lobster," he told me. "I hope that's okay."

"Can I eat it now?"

"If you want, but it'll be kind of hard without any silverware. However, I also have this." Reaching into the bag, he pulled out something wrapped in foil and handed it to me.

I opened it to find Irish soda bread inside. "I could kiss you right now," I told him. Then I shoved a large piece of it into my mouth before I thought to offer him any.

He took a piece anyway, and I watched out the window as the lights of the city passed by, smiling to myself at the look on his face.

IN THE WEEKS THAT FOLLOWED, my life with Luca fell into a rhythm. In the mornings, after he spent an hour or so abusing the punching bag in his home gym and had a shower, we had coffee together on the deck off the main floor when the weather was nice. On the rare occasions it rained this far into summer, we would sit in the seating area just inside the patio doors and listen to the thunder rumble across the sky. Those days were my favorite, when the storms made me feel like we were secluded from the rest of the world.

The first few days, Luca would ask me if I wanted to come train with him. Learn to fight.

"So when I overtake you and escape, it won't weigh on your conscience?" I teased.

He just smiled. But it was strained. And not for the first time, I wished I could hear what he was thinking.

But though I exercised on a regular basis and was in pretty good shape, I would always refuse, telling him it was way too early to get that sweaty. I firmly believed getting up before the sun was a sin against god, and this man was awake a good hour before dawn every day.

In reality, that was only part of the reason I never took him up on his invitation to workout with him, but it was the only one I gave him. However, I didn't want to pass up this opportunity. If I was going to be in his world, it would probably behoove me to learn to protect myself. So instead, I asked him if either of my guards could teach me. After a long pause, he volunteered the larger of the two for the job. Enzo. Mr. Incognito.

When I asked him if he would teach me, he readily agreed. Three times a week he would take me into the gym and "attack" me, making me go through the motions of self-defense techniques over and over until it became second nature. When I asked Enzo why he was bothering to take the time to teach me, he just shrugged and told me more women should know how to fight, whether they lived in the world of the mafia or not.

Enzo pushed me to my limits and then demanded even more, but I found I enjoyed learning to fight. It gave me a sense of empowerment when I managed to land him on the mat at my feet. Perhaps Luca would've been a little easier on me, but maybe not. In any case, I would always wait to train until he was either in his office or gone from the house because I couldn't be in that room with him without remembering.

Today, I was there alone, going over a few combinations Enzo had taught me the day before. I stopped to rest in front of the wall of mirrors, my hands on my knees as I tried to catch my breath. I was pushing myself hard, hoping I'd wear myself out enough to sleep through the night.

When I could breathe, I straightened and immediately caught my reflection in the panel before me. Gingerly, I probed my throat with the tips of my fingers, instantly caught up in the memories of Luca's hand wrapped around it, cutting off my air supply. I stood that way, transfixed by the images in my mind, until something shifted in my peripheral vision. My eyes shot to the side as my hand fell away.

Luca stood in the doorway, watching me. His jacket was off, his tie was gone, and his hair was disheveled, like he'd been running his fingers through it. As soon as I noticed him there, he stepped back into the shadows of the hallway, but not before I saw the ravaged expression on his face. Soon after, I heard his quiet footsteps retreating back down the hallway.

I hoped it unsettled him as much as it did me. The remembering. But I didn't think I would ever know.

That night he came to my room, and I almost sobbed in relief. It was the first time he'd done so since he'd gotten shot. I'd pushed him away, insisting on my own room, but I never thought he'd actually allow it. And other than his claiming of me at the restaurant, he hadn't tried to touch me. My plan seemed to be falling apart, and I didn't know how to get us back to the place we were. We talked every day, in a detached sort of way. But it wasn't enough. And every time I tried to get close to him physically, even just touching his arm or his hand, he would come up with an excuse and leave me, cold and alone.

But not this night.

Without a word, he lifted the covers and got in beside me. Careful of his still healing shoulder, he pulled me against him and wrapped his legs and arms around me. I waited for him to say something. To start touching me. But he didn't. He just took a shaky breath, and ever so slowly, I felt his body relax against mine.

When I woke the next morning, he was gone.

CHAPTER 23
LUCA

"Maybe there's another way, Luca."

I glanced up from my phone to see Enzo watching me in the rearview mirror, his sunglasses on the dash. We were on our way to see my father. I'd left Tristan at the house to keep an eye on Veda. "Another way for what?"

"Another way to get revenge on Mario that doesn't involve an innocent woman."

"You should be watching the road," I told him, dismissing his concerns. I was growing tired of this conversation.

"Luca."

With a heavy sigh, I set aside my phone and the article I'd been reading. "There are many other ways I could be dealing with Mario. But none will bring me so much pleasure as to watch the sheer horror on his face when he realizes I'm about to kill the woman he thinks I took from him."

"Except she's not Nicole Calbert. She's Veda."

He said nothing more. He didn't have to. "You're getting soft, Enzo. Maybe I shouldn't have let you spend so much time with her."

"That's bullshit, and you know it."

We came up to a light, and he stopped the car. Our eyes clashed in the rearview mirror. I met his glare without flinching.

"You care about her," he told me. "More than care about her. And don't try to fucking deny it because I *know* you, Luca. And you're just gonna stick a bullet in her head?"

"Yes," I said without hesitation.

The light turned green, but he didn't go until the car behind us honked their horn. With a curse, he checked his mirrors and stepped on the gas. "There's gotta be another way."

"You think Mario shouldn't get what's coming to him?" I asked in genuine curiosity. "That he shouldn't pay for making a fool out of me in front of our family? For taking away one of the few people in my life I ever dared to care about?"

"I didn't say that."

"Then what exactly are you saying, Enzo?"

"I'm saying she shouldn't have to die for our sick little games. That's all. That maybe, just maybe, there's another way."

"And then what?" I cocked my head to the side. "What the fuck do we do with her then? We can't let her go. She knows too much about us."

"We keep her."

I barked out a laugh, but it was an ugly sound. "We can't keep her."

"Why not?"

"Because she is the one thing that makes me weak," I admitted quietly.

Enzo stared straight ahead. If he felt validated in any way that I'd admitted it out loud, he didn't show it. And he didn't bring up the subject again. There was no point. There was no place for weakness in the type of life I led. He knew this as well as I.

My cell phone vibrated on the seat beside me. It was Tristan. When I looked up, I found Enzo watching me, one eyebrow lifted in question. "That was Tristan," I told him. "We have a lead on Mario's exact whereabouts."

Enzo's eyes dropped back to the road. After a moment, he nodded and slid his sunglasses back on. Nothing more was said by either of us as we turned onto my father's road and went through his security detail.

We were personally greeted by my father at the door of his Texas residence when we arrived. He'd bought the house shortly after I'd moved here, so he'd have a place to stay on his frequent visits. It was only a slightly smaller version of the isolated mansion he owned up north. "Luca! My son! It's about damn time." Grabbing my face in both hands, he kissed each cheek in turn. Then did the same to Enzo. "Enzo, how are you, boy?"

Enzo removed his sunglasses and slid them into the inside pocket of his suit jacket. "I'm good, sir. Thank you."

"Come in! Come in! Linda made pasta."

My father's latest whore came out of the kitchen right on cue, wiping her hands on a towel. Her brassy hair was piled on top of her head, and she wore the usual thick layer of makeup on her face that made her look ten years older than she was, but at least she wore clothes that decently covered her this time, even if the tight pants and top appeared to be two sizes too small. With the allowance my father paid her to stay with him, you would think she could afford to class herself up a bit.

"It's almost ready!" she said with a smile. "Would anyone like a drink?"

"I can get our drinks," my father told her. "Get your ass back in the kitchen. I'm fucking starving. And don't burn the garlic bread this time!" he yelled after her as she skittered away, the smile plastered to her face far less genuine than when she first came out.

"Wine? Or whiskey?" my father asked.

"Whiskey," I told him.

After inviting Enzo to stay and drink, we followed him into the den. Like the rest of his home decor, this room was old-school mafia, all dark wood and red furniture with priceless paintings and collector's items decorating the walls and bookshelves. If anyone ever had the balls to break in here, they'd be set for life, if they managed to live long enough to enjoy it.

"I heard some shit went down at your uncle's birthday between you and Gio. I'm sorry I missed it. My gout was acting up and I couldn't travel." Handing Enzo and me our drinks, he walked back over to the side table to get his and then took a seat in his favorite chair, leaving us the loveseat.

Gout, my ass. The only thing this man suffered from was an aversion to his younger brother. "I should've shot him," I said. "He was being an ass. And I honestly don't think anyone would miss him. Not even his mother."

"He attacked a woman in the bathroom," Enzo filled in. "Luca's woman, to be precise."

"She's not my woman," I corrected him. "She's my revenge. And I can't afford to lose her before we can draw out Mario."

"My mistake," Enzo told me, raising his glass in apology. But I didn't miss the smirk he made no attempt to hide before he took a drink.

I narrowed my eyes at him but didn't remark on it. Turning back to my father, I said, "What Enzo said is true, though. And Gio doesn't know anything except that she's the woman I'm currently involved with. He pulled her into the men's room and touched her inappropriately. But she gave back as good as she got and managed to get away from him right as I found them." Something warmed my chest as I said it. A sense of pride, perhaps.

"Where are we with your plan?" my father asked. "How close are you to finding Mario?"

"I received a message from Tristan while we were on our way over here," I told him. "He has a lead. Mario will be back in the city this weekend from wherever he's been hiding. I told him to let me know as soon as he knows more."

"And you're absolutely positive your pain in the ass brother has no idea his fiancée *is* actually dead. Because if you walk into another trap, Luca, it'll be you who's dead. Your brother won't miss a second time."

It surprised me to see a flicker of concern cross my father's face before it was once again hidden by the unfeeling mask I'd known my entire life. "Rene took care of that mess personally. As you know, he's very thorough. I trust him completely. He wants justice for his sister just as much as I do."

He nodded, but I got the feeling he wasn't satisfied with my answer.

"Even if he put a bullet in Nicole himself, hearing that she's suddenly risen from the dead will be enough to bring him out of hiding. He won't be able to resist seeing it for himself. All I need is a face to face."

My father leaned back in his chair. "And you'll get it. Mario called me right before you arrived. He wants to meet with me."

"What did you tell him?"

"I told him I didn't trust him as far as I could throw his snitching ass and the answer was no. However, after I let him snivel for a bit, I agreed to send one of my men to hear what he had to say." He eyed me over the rim of his glass. "You will be that man."

I held myself perfectly still, not one shred of the myriad of emotion I felt showing on my face. "Just let me know when and where."

Linda called us in to dinner then, and we changed our conversation to less important matters. My father liked to fuck her, but he didn't trust her, which was smart. Women like Linda were only loyal to whoever threw the most money at them. Right now, it was my father, but that could change at any given moment.

After dinner, we had another drink and wrapped up our business. Shortly after, Enzo and I made our excuses and left. It didn't surprise me at all that my father hadn't asked about the gunshot in my shoulder or how I was healing. Perhaps when I was dead, he would shed a tear over my grave. Until then, I was nothing more than his underboss, a position I held onto by the skin of my teeth until I could earn back the respect of the family.

"So, the plan worked," Enzo said once we were back on the road. "Your brother is coming home."

"I never had any doubt."

"Who do you think is feeding the information to Mario?"

"It could be anyone," I told him. "I took her out in public twice. Anyone could have seen us. Hell, Enzo, I was shot after the first time I took her downtown."

"Yeah, I guess you're right."

"What are you trying to get at here?"

He shrugged one shoulder. "I was hoping we could find a reason to nail your cousin as a snitch."

"Gio?" I asked.

"Yeah. The asshole."

Immediately, I shook my head. "Nah. He's no snitch. An asshole with a limited lifespan if he keeps acting the way he does, yes. But not a snitch."

"I'd just feel better if we knew who it was that was relaying info to Mario, starting with the day he barged into your deal with the cartel."

That was a good question, wasn't it?

Tristan met us at the door when we arrived back at the lake house.

"We've got him," I told him.

"Mario?"

I nodded and filled him in on what we'd discussed with my father. "He has a meeting in four days where he thinks he's meeting with our father, but instead, he'll be meeting with one of his men."

He smiled. "You."

"And 'Nicole'."

Tristan exchanged a glance with Enzo. "Ok, then."

Four days. I had four days left with Veda. Four days before I could wipe the smile off my brother's face with a bullet.

I heard a noise above us and looked up to find Veda hastily rising to her feet, her long hair pulled back and a book in her hand. "Let's take this into the office," I told them, dragging my eyes away from her white face.

I cursed under my breath as we relocated to my office, where I began to pace. I took a deep breath. I couldn't let my...attachment to Veda fuck with me. Not now. This had to be done. My life and the life of my friends hung in the balance. I leaned back against my desk. "Okay. Let's go over the plan."

I'd left the door open, half expecting her to follow us, to try to stop me, to give me a reason not to do this. One I couldn't argue my way out of.

But she never appeared.

CHAPTER 24

VEDA

F our days.

I only had four days to make Luca change his mind.

I paced the hall upstairs, the book in my hand forgotten. Maybe I was wrong. Maybe it was something else they were talking about. It was totally possible, right?

But no, I'd distinctly heard Mario's name. And how many Marios could there be?

Well, there was only one way to find out.

Taking a shaky breath, I peered down over the railing, looking for Lisa, but I didn't see her. Hoping she'd gone on an errand, I snuck quietly down the stairs on bare feet and tiptoed down the hall to Luca's office. As I approached, I saw the door had been left open and I could hear voices inside. I stopped as soon as I was close enough to overhear what they were saying, balancing on the balls of my feet and ready to run into the closest room to hide as soon as they stopped talking.

"...sure we can trust your connection? He's not bringing an army with him?" Luca was asking.

"I would bet my life on it," Tristan answered. "Matteo has his own reasons to take Mario out."

"What would those reasons be?"

"I'm sorry, Luca. It's not my place to tell you what they are, but I trust him completely."

There was a pause. "Then that's all I need to know," Luca said.

If I lived through this, I was going to find out who the hell this Matteo dude was and make him rethink his life choices.

"So, we get there a little early, scope out the place," Tristan said.

I could tell by the change of volume in his voice he was looking in my direction. My pulse pounded in my ears, making it harder to hear. Sweat trickled down my spine, and I had to fight the urge to flee. He couldn't see me. And I heard no footsteps. He was probably just confirming with Enzo. But my muscles stayed tense. Ready. Just in case.

"We'll let you know when it's safe to come in with Veda. And at the appointed time, you come in and do what needs to be done. You know the rest."

I didn't know the rest. What the hell is the rest?

My heart was now beating so loudly that I was positive they could hear it. Surely, this couldn't be happening. I firmly believed that Luca was not as cold-blooded as he tried to make everyone think. Even though he'd been pulling away from me these last few weeks, I've seen him. *Really* seen him. Deep down, he feels things. He was not a monster.

I had to believe that. I had to believe that, or the terror would overwhelm me.

"I'll be ready," Luca tells him. "And so will she."

No. No, I won't. My feet were moving, heading toward his office, not bothering to try to be quiet anymore. I found myself standing in the doorway.

Three sets of eyes swung my way, but I only saw Luca. "What exactly is it that I'll be ready for?" I asked him.

"Leave us," Luca told Tristan and Enzo without taking his eyes from me. "Take the night off. We'll talk about this more tomorrow."

They walked out of the office without a word, Enzo closing the door behind him. "But who will watch me tonight?" I asked him. "Aren't you afraid I'll throw myself from the balcony or something?"

"I will," he told me.

I walked closer to him, stopping just out of his reach. "What's happening in four days, Luca?"

He stared at me in silence, his blue eyes cold as steel. No matter how hard I searched, I couldn't find any part of the man I'd gotten to know within them.

I shook my head, refusing to believe I'd been so duped. He was in there somewhere. He had to be. "You can't really mean to go through with this." My voice was little more than a whisper.

"I told you what this was right from the beginning," he finally said. "Don't stand there and act like you didn't know this was coming, Veda. Nothing has changed."

I took a step closer. The book I'd found was still in my hands. I wanted to knock him over the head with it. "How can you say that? Everything has changed."

"Not for me."

His words hit me hard, knocking the air from my lungs. The room around me went in and out of focus. The book fell from my hands, landing on the floor with a thud. Neither of us so much as looked at it.

"Nothing has changed, Veda," he said again. His voice was cold. His demeanor perfectly calm.

All of my efforts, everything I'd done, everything I'd given, meant absolutely nothing to him. I could see this now. And with that realization, the terror I'd managed to keep at bay up until now took over. Tremors began in my hands and moved up my arms, spreading through my body until I stood there trembling uncontrollably. The game had been turned around on me. I hadn't moved him. Didn't change his mind. The only one who gave a shit here was me. Turning on my heel, I walked out of his office, refusing to let him see how he was tearing me apart.

"Veda."

I heard him call my name, but I didn't respond. I had to get to my room. Had to be alone so I could try to process what was about to happen. So I could get my affairs together. I didn't know exactly what Luca had planned for me. I only knew I wouldn't live through it.

In four days.

"Veda!"

I started to run, but not toward the stairs as I'd originally planned. I needed air. I couldn't breathe. I had to get out of this house. The dam inside of me burst and I choked on a sob, tears blurring my vision as I smashed into the front door, my shaking hand fumbling with the locks.

Finally, I managed them and yanked the door open, only to get hit hard from behind. The door slammed shut again as I was thrown against it, knocking the breath from my lungs as my face bashed into the wood. Luca pressed against me as I gasped for air. And in some sick part of my head, I realized I could feel the hard length of him against my ass through my pajama shorts.

"Where the fuck do you think you're going?" His voice was deceptively calm. "You think I'm just gonna let you run out there barefoot, wearing what you're wearing, for my men to find you? Because that's what would happen, *amore*. You wouldn't get halfway to the road before they had you rounded up. The only thing that would keep them from shooting you on sight is if they decided that sweet ass was worth having first."

"Just let me go," I pleaded. "I don't want to play anymore." He pulled me away from the door, turning me in his arms and holding me close against him. I realized I was still trembling. With fear? With desire? I had no way of knowing anymore.

"Shhh..." he told me. Leaving one arm around my back, he ducked down and caught me behind the knees, lifting me effortlessly into his strong arms.

Wrapping my arms around him, I tucked my face into his neck. "I don't want to play anymore. Luca, I don't want to play anymore..."

I repeated the mantra as he carried me up the stairs and into his room. I whispered it as he stripped me of my clothing, his hands touching me everywhere, like he was trying to memorize my body from the top of my head all the way to the soles of my feet. I moaned it as his lips found my breasts, teasing my nipples with his tongue and teeth. I screamed it as he laid me on the bed and spread my legs, his mouth hot and wet on my cunt.

It was only when he rose up and pressed his way into me, forcing my body to accept him, that I stopped pleading and wrapped my arms and legs around him to hold him close to me.

Knowing our time together was running out.

***

I didn't see Luca again after that sleepless night. He left me alone to wander the house and ponder my death while he went about his business, preparing for his meeting with my sister's fiancé.

Was he even thinking about me?

Would he miss me?

Twice, I tried to escape out the door. And once I was halfway over the railing of the balcony in my room before I was caught. Each time, Tristan or Enzo calmly brought me back inside and watched me as I crumbled to the floor in defeat. They never said a word. Didn't try to console me. Just stood by as I worked through my anger and grief.

On the third day, I stopped trying. I decided if I was going to die, I wanted Luca to be the one to do it. I wanted him to look me in the eyes as he pulled the fucking trigger.

On the fourth day, I was lying in bed when Luca came into my room, dressed in black dress pants and a black button-down shirt, his gun holstered under his left arm. I hadn't slept the night before and I couldn't bring myself to eat. I couldn't even force myself to get up.

He didn't bother to knock. "I need you to get up and get a shower. I'm taking you out." There was no emotion in his voice.

I didn't know exactly where he was taking me, but I couldn't see why it mattered if I was clean or not. If I were to guess, probably to some abandoned warehouse out in the middle of nowhere where no one would hear the gunshot or see my blood spilled all over the floor. Did he want to get one last fuck out of me before he offed me?

The pathetic thing that I'd become, this woman who was desperate to live, to grasp at anything that made her feel alive...she would let him.

Walking over to the closet, he pulled out a sapphire blue, one shoulder mini dress that had a diagonal split across my torso from my collarbone to my opposite hip bone. Luckily, the entire thing was tight and hugged my curves. But I still wouldn't jump around in it for fear my boobs would fall right out. I'd tried it on on a whim, and Luca had insisted I get it. So I did. For him. Even though it wasn't like anything I would normally wear.

It was, however, exactly like something my sister, Nicole, would wear.

"Get up, Veda."

Was I imagining it? Or was his voice gentler now than before?

Luca laid the dress on the chair near the closet and came over to me, sitting on the side of the bed so my body curved around his hip.

I stared straight ahead, watching the sun through the window as it began its downward descent over the lake.

Luca had been right when he'd told me it was one of the most beautiful views in Austin. The sky was so big in Texas. The colors so vibrant. It was one of the things I loved about living here.

Out of the corner of my eye, I saw him lift his hand toward me, saw it hover in the space between us for just a second before he tangled his fingers in my hair. His touch was gentle as he brushed it back from my face. Like a lover would touch someone they cared about deeply. But it was a lie. It was all a lie. Every look. Every touch. "Come on, *amore*. Get out of this bed. I want to take you out."

"I don't want to go," I whispered.

"I know," he said. "But I need you."

He wasn't going to leave. So I had two choices. I could get up and do as he asked, or I could lay here and refuse. In which case he would get me up, drag me to the shower, and get me dressed anyway. Then he'd take me out of the house, kicking and screaming, but out I would go.

With a sigh, I decided I'd rather save my dignity, so I rolled over to the other side of the bed and got up.

An hour later, I walked down the stairs in the dress he'd picked out for me, complimented with a pair of strappy gold heels. My hair was down the way he liked it, and I'd put on a little makeup. My eyes were blue.

Luca watched me, his heated gaze traveling slowly from the top of my head to the tips of my toes and back again. "You're stunning," he told me when I walked up to him.

I didn't reply. His compliment meant nothing to me. I felt nothing. I cared about nothing.

"Tristan and Enzo are waiting in the car."

He placed his hand on my lower back and led me outside to the SUV, opening the door for me and helping me climb into the backseat before closing it behind me. I had my seatbelt on when he got in beside me. "Let's go," he told Enzo.

Enzo caught my eye in the rearview mirror, and for a moment, I thought he was going to say something. But then he picked up his sunglasses from the dash and put them on.

I glanced over at Tristan. His expression was hard as stone as he stared straight out the windshield.

The trip into the city went by way too fast, and before I knew it, we were in north Austin. I looked out the window. A club? Luca was bringing me to a club full of people?

He opened the door for me and held out his hand. "Come on, let's have some fun."

Confused, and not knowing what else to do, I took his hand and got out of the car, careful not to flash anyone even though Enzo and Tristan were standing in front of us with their backs to the car, scanning the crowd of people in line to get inside.

Wrapping his arm tight around my waist, Luca walked us to the front of the line. A large bouncer with dark skin and multiple facial piercings took one look at Luca, gave us a nod, and unhooked the rope, letting us skip the line. Enzo and Tristan follow us in.

I looked back over my shoulder as the door closed behind me, catching the last lingering rays of the sunset, unsure if I'd ever see those colors again.

CHAPTER 25
VEDA

I'd never made an ass of myself in a club this nice before, but that's exactly what I planned to do tonight. If I was about to leave this world, I was going out with a bang. And this was the perfect dress to do it in.

The place had three levels. On the main level, where we were, women wearing scraps of material just barely wide enough to keep them legal hung upside down from ropes high above the heads of the crowd on the dance floor, shifting to new poses along with the music before twirling to "oohs" and "ahhs" from the crowd below. A man in tails and a top hat on top of the bar misted the dancers to keep them cool, and shot girls in sexy tuxedo shirts and tight black shorts and heels walked around with sparklers stuck in the corners of the trays they carried.

Above us were more tables overlooking the dance floor at a level with the acrobats. And on either side of the club, just inside the front doors, stairs led down to a third level.

As we walked past, I quickly looked away, not wanting to know what happened down there.

After Luca dropped five hundred cash to secure us a table behind the roped off area right off the dance floor, I flagged down the waitress, not caring if I seemed rude. Yelling above the heavy beat of the dance mix playing, I ordered a lemon drop martini and a shot of their best tequila.

"Make that two shots."

I looked over to find Luca holding out a hundred-dollar bill toward the pretty, dark-haired, brown-eyed waitress, but his eyes were on me.

"And keep them coming," he told her.

"Yes, sir." Taking the cash, she moved to the next table, where Enzo and Tristan sat with their backs to the wall.

As we waited for our drinks, I watched the dancers, trying desperately to keep my mind off of what was going to happen, and failing miserably. By the time the waitress showed up with my alcohol, I was trembling violently and having trouble breathing. Tequila spilled over the edge of the shot glass as I lifted it to my lips with a shaking hand, and I nearly cried with relief when the nasty stuff burned its way down my throat, warming my insides just enough to keep me from breaking down completely. I wished I'd never overheard them talking. I wished I didn't know this was the night I was going to die. That this was only Luca giving me one last night out.

"Veda."

I turned my head to find him in the chair right beside me. I searched his face, silently begging him to tell me everything was okay. That he'd changed his mind. Hell, maybe even that he loved me. But he said none of those things.

Blue eyes seared my skin everywhere they roamed, from my eyes to my lips and lower, to my breasts and even my legs, burning with something I didn't understand. Unable to take the intensity of his gaze, I tried to turn away, but his hand shot up and gripped my jaw, forcing me to look at him.

Slowly, his thumb rubbed my bottom lip, smearing my lipstick as the tears I could no longer contain slipped silently down my cheeks.

His mouth came down on mine, hard and hungry. He tasted like salt and tequila, and my hands came up to grip his shirt. I meant to push him away, I did. But that's not what happened. Instead, I hung on tight. Like maybe if I could hang on tight enough, he could keep me here with him.

Breaking off the kiss, he kept his hand on my jaw, holding me still as he put his mouth near my ear. "You make me weak, *vita.*" He pulled back just enough to bring his face into focus. Still holding my jaw, he brought up the fingers of his other hand, shoving one into my mouth and rubbing something bitter on my gums. He pressed a hard, fast kiss to my bruised lips and released me.

I began to panic and tried to rub off whatever he'd just put in my mouth, but he grabbed my wrists and held them in my lap. "Leave it."

"What is that?" I yelled over the music.

When he saw my terrified reaction, he frowned and took my face between his hands, forcing me to still. "Shhh...just relax," he told me. "It's just something to help you have a good time."

I tried to get my racing thoughts under control. "You drugged me?" I didn't do drugs. Never had. The one time I'd tried to smoke pot, I'd hated the way I'd felt the entire time and had sworn off everything except an occasional alcoholic beverage ever since.

He brushed my hair off my face in that way he always did. "It's okay," he told me. "You'll like it. Trust me."

Trust me.

I started to laugh. I couldn't help it. That was the most absurd thing I'd ever heard in my short life.

Luca suddenly stood. "Come on." Taking my hand, he brought me to my feet, then leaned down and said something to Enzo. He nodded and stood also, but didn't follow us as Luca led us out onto the dance floor and took me into his arms. His left hand took my right, tucking it beneath his jacket against his hard chest as his other hand splayed wide on my lower back.

Even in my heels, the top of my head barely came to his jaw, and I felt small and insignificant in the crowd of people. I held myself stiff at first, concentrating only on holding back the screams that threatened to burst free. But gradually, I gave in to the music pulsing through my veins as we swayed to the beat in the small space we were allotted by the crowd.

Luca was an amazing dancer. Or maybe I was just high. Either way, it didn't really matter. I don't know how long we were out there. I only knew that with every minute that passed I relaxed more and more, my body molding to his like I was meant to be a part of him. I found myself smiling as I tilted my head back and watched the lights spin around us. Something warm and wet touched the side of my neck. His lips and tongue. It felt good, so I moved my head to give him better access.

His hand slid down until he was cupping my ass, and he pulled my hips closer until I could feel him against my stomach, hot and hard and swollen. I slid my hand around the back of his neck, holding his mouth to my skin as he bent me back right there in the middle of the dance floor, his lips and tongue burning a trail over my collarbone and lower, until he was stopped by the material of my dress. With a growl I felt more than heard, he tugged at it with his teeth.

"Luca," I moaned. I wanted him. Right there on the fucking dance floor. I didn't give a shit who watched. But apparently, Luca did, for he suddenly righted me so fast the room spun and I almost fell on my ass. However, his arms were still around me, holding me up until I could do it on my own.

And then we were moving, dancing our way through the crowd. I laughed with delight as he maneuvered us through the throng of dancers, shoving people out of the way with one arm when they wouldn't move.

The next thing I knew, we were in a dark hallway and Luca had me pressed up against the wall. His mouth came down on mine. Hard. Hungry. Wiping everything from my mind but what was happening this moment. His hands were on my outer thighs, lifting my skirt so high I knew anyone who walked back there would see my navy lace underwear.

"Touch me, *amore*."

He sounded desperate, almost pleading, and euphoria swept through me to hear it, to know he needed me like I needed him. When I got too caught up in the colors of my thoughts and didn't react fast enough, he grabbed my hand and pressed it against his cock. My fingers locked around him, and I was rewarded when Luca tangled his fingers in my hair, tilting my head so he could ravage my mouth.

Footsteps sounded to my left, and before I knew what was happening, Luca had his gun pointed at the guy, his other hand still wrapped in my hair and my hand still around his cock. "Find another fucking bathroom," he growled.

I giggled as the guy put up his hands and slowly backed away. Jesus Christ, what the hell was wrong with me?

Oh, yeah. I was drugged.

We were moving again. Luca walked me backward through a doorway, kicking it shut with his foot. I glanced around and saw a sink with a long, black counter next to a couple of open stalls. Urinals lined the opposite wall.

The heavy beat of the music pulsed through speakers in the ceiling. The fluorescent light above us flickered, only one dim bulb still working. But for a men's room, it wasn't as gross as I'd expected.

Luca's hands were in my hair, and his mouth came back to mine. My lips were already swollen and bruised, but I wrapped my arms around his neck, kissing him back with all the love in my heart. I felt absolutely euphoric. I knew it was the drugs, but I didn't care. At this moment, I wanted to believe the illusion.

He kissed me until I couldn't breathe, his hands traveling over my back and down to my ass and back again. My blood surged to the surface, sensitizing my skin until I could feel every tiny nuance of his touch. I wanted to be naked. To feel the soft material of his suit against my skin. I could've been kissing him for seconds or hours. I had no idea. I just knew it felt so fucking good...

With a desperate moan, he pulled away. "I'm sorry," he told me.

Before I could ask him what he was sorry about, he spun me around and placed both of my palms flat on the counter on either side of the sink. He kicked my feet apart, spreading my legs, then he pulled my hips back. My lace panties were ripped from my body. His hands were on my thighs, and I felt the cold air from the A/C on my bare ass and the head of his cock sliding through the folds of my pussy. I shivered with expectation, every nerve in my body tingling. There was pressure as he pushed inside of me, giving me no time to adjust to his size. I gasped as he pulled out just a little, then pushed in again, a little further this time.

Lifting my head, I watched him in the mirror as he worked his way inside of me. His jaw was clenched. His eyes on my ass. When he finally slid all the way in, I couldn't stop the moan that escaped me. Blue eyes shot up, meeting mine in the mirror, and I was shocked at what I saw there.

Sorrow. Desperation. Anger.

Before I could ask him what was wrong, he dropped his eyes and started to move. His fingers dug into my hips as he slammed into me from behind, fast and hard, until it was all I could do to stay on my feet in these damn heels. He fucked me like he was trying to exorcise a demon, and maybe he was.

Bending forward, he reached around me and pulled down the material of my dress, exposing my breast and pinching my nipple hard. I cried out at the pain, but it was followed by a swift surge of desire as I heard him growl behind me.

On and on, he fucked me, his hands on my ass, my hips, my breasts, my shoulders...until my arms and legs were shaking from trying to hold myself up. But he didn't relent. If anything, he fucked me harder.

"Veda..." My name was a plea on his lips, and then he slammed into me one more time as he cried out. His arm came around me and I felt the weight of him sag against my back as he braced his other arm on the sink, holding us up.

I felt every drop as he came inside of me, and I'd never felt more a part of him than right now, at this very moment. I didn't come. I didn't have to. I felt our souls touch.

When he could breathe again, Luca pulled out of me, and a sense of loss surged through every cell of my body. "Stay there," he ordered. "Don't move." I watched him in the mirror as he tucked himself back inside his pants. Then he grabbed some paper towels out of the basket on the sink, wet them under the faucet, and stepped behind me. He was gentle as he washed the slickness from pussy and thighs, and when he was done, I straightened, and he helped me pull my dress down.

Luca's phone rang. His eyes met mine as he put it to his ear, and I watched with something akin to fascination as they froze over again, like a slow-motion film of the Caribbean turning into a glacier. The man who had just fucked me so desperately disappeared. "Yes, we're ready."

CHAPTER 26
LUCA

Veda stiffened beside me when she spotted Mario and his men standing side by side on the other side of the back parking lot. She didn't ask me any questions. Didn't beg. Didn't try to weasel her way out of what was about to happen. What *had* to happen. I hoped she was still stoned enough that she wouldn't feel anything. Wouldn't see what was coming.

For me, seeing my brother for the first time since the drug bust had gone down was strange. I expected to feel more. Sorrow, perhaps. Loss for the brother I knew when we were kids, before he had become this selfish prick. But all I felt was a sense of betrayal. And an anger that threatened to consume me.

Mario immediately spotted Veda standing calmly beside me, and the blood drained from his face. His eyes flicked back to me. "What is this? I'm supposed to meet one of our father's men."

"That would be me," I told him.

His eyes were pulled back to Veda. "This isn't possible. They told me it was her, but I didn't fucking believe it." He took a step toward us. Stopped. "I thought for sure you were just pulling some shit, Luca. Trying to get me to show myself." Then he shook his head, took a step forward, stopped, and pointed his finger at her. "You're dead. I fucking shot you myself." His arm fell to his side, his eyes wide. "This isn't. Fucking. Possible."

"Obviously, you missed." I smiled at the expression on his face, but there was no warmth behind it.

His eyes never left Veda. "What are you fucking doing with him?" I could see the spit spew from his mouth from where we stood. It brought joy to my heart.

Veda just stared at him and didn't respond.

"Answer me, you fucking bitch!"

Anger surged through me at the insult, but I suppressed it. I couldn't lose focus. "I think you just answered your own question, Mario," I told him. "Women like to feel cared for. Respected." Though my voice was calm, my gut clenched so tight I was glad I hadn't been able to bring myself to eat today. I felt Veda staring at me, but I didn't look at her to see her reaction to my words. Grinding my jaw, I shoved down the feeling that I was somehow betraying her. I'd been planning this day for years. *Fucking years.* Veda knew what was coming from the moment she became a guest at my home. I wasn't about to let my fondness for her pussy ruin this for me.

Or for Maria.

My brother finally turned his attention to me. "Is this what you wanted? To steal my girl?" He threw his arms out. "Fine, *stronzo*. You did it. You took something from me. Just like I did to you. Now you can go crawling back to our daddy and tell him what a big man you are."

I laughed. "Don't be stupid, *fratello*," I told him. "I didn't need to 'steal' anything. She came to me willingly." I tightened my hand around her arm in warning when I saw Veda's mouth open out of the corner of my eye. "And who can blame her? You claimed to love her. Told her you were gonna marry her. Then tried to kill her. And for what? For being excited?"

Mario looked to his men on either side of him. "Fine," he said. "We're even now. I took your woman, and you took mine. Can we stop with all of this now so I can get on with my life?"

"Your life?" I barked out a laugh. "You're a fucking *rat*, Mario. You have no *life*."

"So, what?" He put his hands out, palms up. "What are you gonna do, Luca? You gonna kill me? Your own brother?"

I didn't bother to answer him. He knew if that was my plan, he'd already be dead. "I thought maybe you might want her back," I told him. "So you'd have some company the next time you ran to the feds like the pussy you are." Veda made a small noise, but I wouldn't look at her. I couldn't. If I did, if I looked into her eyes and saw the hurt and betrayal and fear I was causing her, I'd never be able to go through with what I was about to do.

"Why the fuck would I want back a used cunt like that?" He emphasized the insult by waving his hand toward her like she was nothing more than a pile of stinking trash.

My vision narrowed, the cars and people around us turning into a red blur, blocking out everything else except my brother.

"Luca," Enzo said quietly, a warning in his voice.

I didn't acknowledge him. I knew what he was telling me. Mario's life was in our father's hands, not mine. As the boss, it was his call. But that didn't mean I couldn't fuck with him a little. "So, you don't care if I shoot her in the head right here in front of you? The way you shot my Maria? Or should I wait until you're fucking her to do it? So you can taste her blood. Have her brains splattered all over your face and chest. Watch the life fade from her eyes while your dick is still inside of her..." I cocked my head, waiting for an answer.

"Oh, my god." The words were spoken so softly I barely heard them above the blood pounding in my ears. "Oh, my god," Veda repeated, a little louder.

Mario didn't even spare her a glance. But I heard the horror in her voice, and I wanted to scream, "NOW do you get it? NOW do you see why I have to do this? NOW do you understand why my feelings for you don't matter?" But I said none of those things. And outwardly no one would know the turmoil that raged inside of me.

As far as anyone else in this room would see, I was cold. Calculating. Intent on my revenge. It was important that Mario see what I was capable of. How deep the ice in my heart ran.

Slowly, I lifted my Glock and put the muzzle against the side of her head, blocking out Veda's whimper and the way she breathed in and out in bursts, like she couldn't get enough air. But I could smell her fear, and it tugged at something inside of me no matter how hard I tried to ignore it.

With an internal shake, I concentrated on my brother. I remembered what he'd done. What it had felt like. The smell of Maria's blood. The feel of her body as she grew cold against me. The way he'd made me look like a fool in front of our father. In front of the family. In front of the cartel. I couldn't lose my focus. Not again.

And though Veda trembled uncontrollably against me, she didn't say another word, or try to get away from me. I had drugged her for just this purpose. I had to stay focused. I couldn't get distracted by her fighting me, trying to run. And, if I were to be honest with myself, to make it easier on her.

Mario, however, took a stunted step forward, raising his hands out in front of him in a pleading gesture as the four guns on either side of him were pointed at me. Enzo and Tristan, who stood just behind and to either side of me, responded in kind.

"Hold on, Luca. Just hold on." Mario's tone was calm, but his expression was tense. Indicating Veda with one hand, he said, "She's got nothing to do with any of this."

I smiled. "But that's where you're wrong," I told him. "She has everything to do with it. Despite what you did, you love her, just like I loved Maria." And he did love her. I could see it written all over his face, no matter how he tried to act otherwise. I knew my brother. He would never propose to someone he didn't care about. He'd come out of hiding for her. Risked his own life. Killing her had been a necessity that had probably torn him up inside more than he would ever admit.

"Maria was a drug runner, for god's sake. She was in the business! Nicole...Nicole is innocent." His expression softened when he looked at her. "Let her go, Luca. We'll settle this another way."

"There is no other way," I told him.

My grip tightened on Veda's arm for a moment, an unconscious reaction. Moving my hand to her back, I gave her a hard shove and sent her stumbling across the concrete.

Mario rushed toward her, coming to an abrupt stop when I raised my gun and aimed it at her head. He threw up his hands, his eyes pleading now. "Luca, please. I'm begging you."

The sense of satisfaction I felt wasn't nearly as strong as I'd imagined it would be, but it was there.

Veda lifted her head, then slowly turned around to face me. Her eyes met mine, and there was acceptance in her gaze. Acceptance and sorrow.

And love.

I gave my head a little shake. No. That couldn't be right. How the fuck could a woman like her love a monster like me? I was seeing things. Trying to give myself a reason not to do it. She was making me fucking soft. Weak. Just like my brother. But I wasn't like him. Not anymore.

Steadying my arm, I took aim at the center of her forehead. I didn't want her to suffer. A gust of warm summer wind blew by, ruffling the soft strands of her hair. I wished I could run my fingers through them one more time.

"I forgive you," she said softly as her eyes grew shiny with tears and one slipped down her cheek. "I want you to know that."

"Don't do that," I whispered. The door I had shut tight on my emotions rattled inside of me. "Don't *fucking* do that."

"I'm so sorry he did that to you." Another tear rolled down her face, and she blinked hard.

I watched that tear travel along the side of her nose to the corner of her sweet lips, still swollen from my kisses, and drip off her jaw. I wanted to taste her pain as I tasted her blood that first night. Take it away from her and inside myself so she wouldn't hurt anymore.

There was a sharp, stabbing pain in my chest. Another crack in the ice I'd held around my heart.

Fuck.

Fuck. Fuck. FUCK.

Shoot her! Just fucking shoot her! I had to go through with this. I had to. If I didn't, I was as good as dead myself. If my brother didn't kill me this time, someone else would, once they knew I had a heart to crush. Veda would end up a pawn in the endless death games the families played. As soon as word got around that she was a weakness for me, she'd be hunted like an animal. My enemies would come after her as a way to get to me, just as I had with Mario. It was how it worked. She would never be safe. She was better off dead now.

"Luca..."

Enzo's urgent tone came to me as if through a fog. I realized the gun was shaking in my hand. No. My hand was shaking. My arm.

"Just do it, Luca," Veda whispered. "It's okay."

But she stared at me with those luminous eyes. The wrong color, but still *her* looking out at me. They drilled everything she was feeling right into my heart. Right into my soul. Goddammit, I could fucking *feel* her inside of me. What would happen when I went through with this? How would I breathe without her beside me?

I caught movement in my peripheral. I shifted my gaze just in time to see Mario make a motion with his hand. He lunged for Veda as shots fired around me.

In slow motion, I swung my arm to the left and pulled the trigger. Mario's right shoulder jerked back as my bullet caught him, but he didn't stop. He kept going, ducking behind Veda like the fucking coward he was and pulling her against him with his good arm as I took aim again.

Something primitive and feral snapped inside of me the moment he dared to touch her, breaking me down and violently shaking me out of the prison of revenge I'd caged myself in.

Ignoring the bullets flying back and forth between my guys and his, we stood at a standoff, my gun still aimed at his head. But I didn't dare shoot.

Mario had one arm around Veda's throat and one around her waist, the tip of his Glock shoved into the bottom of her breast, pointed at her heart. He whispered something in her ear and her eyes widened as they locked onto mine.

I gave her a fast shake of my head. Too fast for anyone but her to see. And I could only hope she understood my meaning and wouldn't let on who she really was. If she told Mario her true identity, she would be dead within the hour.

Tristan grunted to my right, and I felt more than saw him go down to the floor.

"Fuck! Luca, we gotta go," Enzo yelled. "We have to go!" He stepped in front of me, still firing shots. "Get Tristan."

"I'm not leaving here without her," I told him as I stepped around him and fired off a few rounds, catching one of Mario's men off guard. His gun fell to the ground with a clatter of metal on pavement, his arm hanging useless at his side.

A bullet grazed my head, so close I heard the air move above my ear. Lifting my hand, I touched my temple. When I pulled it away, there was blood on my fingers.

Veda's scream cut through the ringing in my ears. Mario was dragging her backward, his men closing ranks around them.

I took a step toward them, getting off two shots before someone hit me from the side, knocking me down to the ground.

"Get back! Get back!" Enzo yelled, his heavy weight holding me down. Grabbing the back of my jacket, he pulled me with him behind a car. "What are you fucking doing?" he asked me.

I didn't answer him. I didn't fucking know what I was doing. All I knew was that that *fucking* bastard, Mario, was taking away the woman I loved.

Again.

"How's Tristan?" A bullet ricocheted near my head, and I ducked behind the tire as Enzo returned fire.

"He's alive," he said.

"Veda?"

A door slammed and tires squealed.

"Gone," Enzo said. "But alive."

I sat there on my ass, breathing hard as Enzo went to check on Tristan. It was suddenly quiet. Too fucking quiet. All I could hear was the pounding of my heart and the voice inside my head telling me I had failed, both Veda and myself.

"He's okay," Enzo shouted. "He was wearing his vest. He's just stunned, and he'll have a hell of a bruise."

Drawing up my knees, I closed my eyes and covered my face with my hands, one still holding my gun. If Mario found out who Veda really was, how I'd deceived him, he would take his fury out on her.

I met Enzo's eyes, and I could see he was having the same thoughts. "I will fucking find her if I have to kill everyone to do it," I told him.

He gave me a nod, and together, we got Tristan out to the car and headed back to the house to plan the second abduction of Veda.

The End of *His Game*.
Continue Luca and Veda's story with *His Stakes*.

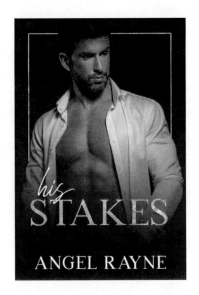

ACKNOWLEDGMENTS

First and foremost, I need to thank my wonderful husband, Joe, for always being my biggest supporter as I venture into this new to me genre. I love you, Joe Joe. <3

To my friend and fellow author, Kristen Strassel, for being excited with me about this new direction and pen name I'm taking. We'll be HRAB's yet!

My bestest author friend, Isabel Jordan, for being my alpha beta reader, talking me off the ledge, always being available to commiserate with me with all of this hard authoring stuff, and holding my hand through blurb hell.

Donna P, for reading this book in its infancy and giving me such valuable feedback. I so appreciate you!

Angel's Army, my ARC team, you all are awesome! Thank you for all of your patience and hanging with me. Your support means the world to me!

And most importantly to YOU, for taking a chance on my books in this new genre. Thank you so, so much for reading.

ABOUT THE AUTHOR

Hi! My name is Angel Rayne and I write dark, delicious romance with antiheroes who would burn down the world to save the woman they love. I never understood why the villains never win the girl, and so I decided to write them their own love stories where they do.

Here are a few other odds and ends about me...

-Music inspires my stories and I make playlists for every book.

-I am not a fast writer. My stories take time to write. They need to brew in my head. To have book releases close together I have to write ahead. But I would much rather take the time the stories need to be the best they can be than try to rush them out. Trust me on this one.

-I love the rain, and I'm happiest when I'm sitting in a coffee shop with my laptop as it storms outside.

-I prefer to go watch movies alone, with one of those fancy coffees hidden in my purse. (Yes, I really do this.)

-My husband calls me his "little bird" because anything that sparkles catches my eye.

-I will never have enough soft blankets. Ever.

-I love ALL THE DRAMA...but only in books.

-I will forever re-watch The Phantom of the Opera with the hope that by some miracle, this time Christine will choose the right guy.

Thank you for reading my stories, and I always love to hear from you! You can reach me at: angel@angelrayne.com

Made in United States
North Haven, CT
24 August 2022

23111535R00200